# Aggie Lichen; Pilp Collector

## Arty's Revenge

### Debra J Edwards

Published by PurpleRay Publishing

PurpleRay Publishing is the book imprint of
Debra J Edwards
info@purpleraypublishing.co.uk
www.purpleraypublishing.co.uk

First printed November 2006
Reprinted 2006

A CIP Record for this book is available from the British
Cataloguing in Publication Data Office

ISBN 0-9550192-1-4

Printed in Bookman Old Style by
York Publishing Services Ltd
www.yps-publishing.co.uk

For Anna, Jackie and Jo.
Their friendship and support never waivers.


For Richard.
Whose help with technical aspects
has been invaluable.


For my readers; Emily, Marie and Elizabeth.
Thank you for your honesty and encouragement.


And for believers everywhere ...

# Chapter One

In fairy terms, it had been six long months since the pilpblast – the annual get together for pilp collectors (we're known as tooth fairies by humans). My straight black hair, which defied all attempts to curl it, had grown even longer and I was at least two millimetres taller! That's a lot as the average pilp collector height was only eighteen centimetres and I was almost sixteen already.

I stood and looked at the mess I called my bedroom. It desperately needed a tidy but it would have to wait as I had the nightsgritch to complete. On those evenings, pilp collectors did the job they were created for; collecting teeth from pilp donors – known, in the human world, as children.

Out of the blue a loud yet muffled voice cut through my thoughts from down the hallway.

'Sorry, Pa. I was away with the humans! What did you say?'

'I said take your sister with you.'

Now where had I heard that before?

'... and take the cauliflower too.'

'I think you mean the cabbage, Pa.'

'Yeah – that too.'

Strange, you may be thinking, being asked to take a cabbage out with you but this cabbage was slightly different to the normal variation of the vegetable. For starters, this cabbage could speak and fly. In fact, this cabbage was not really a cabbage at all. It was actually a small green sprite, who went by the name of Wjdups, or Victor to the non-spritespiel speaking population. He sported the usual sprite characteristics; two large non-blinking eyes, large floppy ears and a humungous mouth.

Now, collecting from pilp donors with the annoying bugfaced sister, also known as Myrtle, I had got used to, but taking a sprite, well that was more than a little strange. For starters, sprites were traditionally the enemies of pilp collectors. The land of Pilpsville had suffered many an invasion of sprites, the last one just before the pilpblast. Victor was part of the sorry mess they'd left behind. He'd somehow got forgotten when the sprites left town and after being found in an old wardrobe, was somewhat reluctant to return to Spercham – spriteland – on his own. And seeing as he was an orphan, well, we kind of just let him stay.

I looked back critically at myself in the mirror and adjusted the hem of my old green dress again. The untidy contents of my shared bedroom reflected back at me with a vengeance. The two huge tree beds were in desperate need of making and clothes were spread around the room like a contagious virus. Between the bulging wooden wardrobes, the dressing table fought for space while the white enamel bricks, from which the whole house was made, still gleamed from Ma's vigorous spring clean and made everything look old and shabby. What a mess!

'zpv sfbez, vhmz?' shouted the cabbage, who incidentally refused to speak in anything but spritepiel.

I put my head around the bedroom door, still half dressed, comb in my hand. 'What? What are you on about?' I asked. 'And put that horrid green tongue back in your head!'

'He said are you ready?' Myrtle emerged from the kitchen, her hand clutching the newly decorated pilp sack Ma had made for her tenth birthday.

'Are you sure that's all he said?'

'Yeah! You should learn spritespiel,' she said, smugly, 'then you'll know exactly what he's saying, won't you?' She flicked her wiry red mop of hair behind her shoulder.

'So it did say something else, huh?'

Myrtle raised her eyebrows to the ceiling. 'And you're supposed to be older and wiser than me, huh?'

Well I was, but only by four years.

'if tbje bsf zpv sfbez, vhmz!' spat the little green cabbage.

'Now what did he say!' I stuck my face into Victor's.

'Oh, I wish you two would stop arguing. I'm sick

of being in the middle,' said Myrtle.

'Huh? Why did he say that?' I said.

'He didn't, stupid, that's what I said!'

'Who are you calling stupid, Bugface?' I gave her a poke just to remind her who was boss in this relationship.

'fs! tuvqje cz obnf, tuvqje cz obuvsf.'

'Oh, shut up, Victor!' we both screamed together.

I'm sure he only came round our house to annoy me. Why'd he bother? I had Bugface to annoy me full time. He still hadn't quite forgiven me for *not* letting the sprites in to invade us!

'Aggie, you ready yet?' bellowed a familiar voice from the back door – Bessie, best friend and fellow pilp collector.

'Nearly there, so stop grumbling,' I shouted as I quickly retreated back inside the bedroom to finish dressing. I quickly discarded my original green dress for another in black. A change of image was badly needed and black could be it.

I hadn't even got as far as putting on my first boot when the door crashed back into the wall causing bits of enamel to fly off in all directions.

There stood Bessie, white faced and shaking wildly. 'Where are they?'

'Where are what?' I said.

'G-G-Grublins! I heard you – you definitely said Grublins.' Bessie's eyes scanned the room for the tell-tale signs; three nostrils, pointed but very small ears, bulging eyes, and not forgetting the strangely cute mouth.

'Crikey, Bess. I'm sure you're getting worse. I said *grumbling* not Grublin. It's about time you made an appointment to see a healer. Do you really think I'd have an arch enemy in the house?'

Victor put his head round the door and sniggered.

'Okay, point taken, cabbage breath! Now get out.'

He disappeared just as the shoe bounced off the door frame.

'I think you're right, Aggie,' said Bessie, mopping her brow and pushing wisps of her thick brown hair away from her face. 'Some of the nightmares I've been having have been awful – ever since the last battle, the day before the pilpblast. That moment on the factory rooftop in Grublin City will live with me forever.' She shivered nervously as she relived the past, 'when all those vile creatures tried to turn us into Grublins with that grey drink. And when they chased us back to Pilpsville ...'

'Stop it, Bess! You're getting in a state again.' I handed her the brown paper bag always kept at close proximity for such 'Bessie' occasions. 'Come on, deep breaths into the bag. You know the routine.' In an effort to convince her further, I threw open the wardrobe door for inspection. 'Look, no Grublins.'

As she sat on the end of my bed calming herself

down, I tied the laces of my black boots and carefully re-arranged my fringe in front of the mirror, once more.

'You look different today,' she mumbled from inside the brown bag, casting her eyes disapprovingly over my all black attire. 'Did somefairy die?'

'Er doh! No, you twit – I'm a goff,' I said proudly, twanging my black bracelet near her ear.

'Er doh! Humans are goffs, not fairies. You pick up far too many bad habits from them, Aggie Lichen!' She cast her eyes around the room which reflected many aspects of the human world.

'Anyway, look at you with your, with your, em, gungy look!' I said, pulling at the long pink flowery dress and brown knitted jacket, handmade, as were all Bessie's clothes, by her granma.

Her eyes laughed and after taking one last deep breath into the bag before discarding it in the litter bin, she seemed back to her *normal* self. 'Right, that's better – oh, before I forget, Gertie Cruet's back in town after *'recuperating from her terrible ordeal'* as she put it.'

Great! The school bully returns to wreak havoc once more.

Bessie continued, 'and she gave me a message to give to you. Hmmm, now how did it go, ah yes ...' She fluffed out her thick curly hair and stuck out her chin in typical Gertie fashion. 'Hmm Hmm, "Tell that bloody Lichen that I'm so gonna get her back for what she did to me at the pilpblast." I think she was a bit upset.'

'What I did? Bugface put the Grublin potion in her drink, not me!'

'Hey,' shouted Bessie, holding her hands up in the air. 'I'm just the messenger.'

'I know, I know.' I splurted a giggle. 'Oh my wings – she looked so funny. What a great Grublin she made – shame she didn't stay like it!' I sighed deeply, 'but now she's back, she'll wait and wait for an opportunity and then ...'

'Oh, don't worry about her. She's all mouth – and hair. Come on! We'll miss the crossing.' And with that, she marched out of the bedroom as if nothing had ever happened.

'We never miss the crossing!' I shouted after her knowing full well that if the crossing portal to the other side closed, there'd be no pilp collecting for us tonight.

'Okay, I'm nearly done. I just need to find my pilp sack then I'll definitely be ready,' I shouted.

'Aggie, hurry up,' said Bugface, running past the bedroom door to get to the kitchen.

'zfbi, zpv bmxbzt mbtu vhmz gbjsz,' added Victor.

'You'd better shut him up, before I ...'

A loud knock at the front door diffused the

tension. More so called friends come to hassle me, no doubt.

'I said I'm ready...'

The huge wooden front door swung open noisily, crashing against the wall, deepening the gash in the enamel further.

'What are you, deaf or something?' I shouted, not paying full attention to the caller.

The sudden sight of small shell buttons hanging on for dear life to a very large checked jacket signalled that the even larger owner of said jacket was neither deaf or, indeed, something.

'Ah, Mr Fettock. Er, I didn't know it was you.' The Headmaster of both Pilpsville Major and Pilpsville Minor School looked on bemused. 'I don't normally, er, shout at doors like that although technically I wasn't shouting at the door, I was shouting at you ...'

Why didn't he say something and stop my mouth from rambling on? It continued ...

'... but I wasn't shouting at you as such, I was shouting at the fairy knocking at the door which in this case was ... you!'

'So you were shouting at me then?' he said, forcing a semi-smile.

Damn! There should be a limit to the amount of rubbish a mouth can spurt out involuntarily.

'Never mind all that, Lichen. I've come here to congratulate you and your family ...'

'Er, sorry, I'm not quite with you.' My heart skipped a beat. At last! Six months late but could it be the long awaited gold medal of honour for courage and …

'I said I've come to congratulate you and your family.' The hair that straddled his bald head flapped around excitedly in the breeze.

'Congratulate us? On what?' I said, puffing up my chest proudly. This could be it, I could see it now …

'Well it just so happens that your numbers have come up …'

Oh well, down to Mirvellon with a bump! 'Sorry, Mr Fettock but our numbers have come up on what exactly?'

'The monthly draw …'

'The monthly draw?' I repeated.

'Yes, you know, the draw that's made monthly hence its title – the monthly draw!'

'But …' A large gulp came to my throat sending my brain into overload. Surely he didn't mean … impossible – we can't have – no, must be some kind of joke – but he wasn't laughing.

'I think there must be some mistake,' I said, anxiously. 'We stopped buying tickets ages ago after the prizes were changed – after the prizes started to … well, after the prizes started to answer back.'

He looked at me and tutted. 'Dear, dear, Lichen, I'm surprised at you, after all you've done for the community too …'

Mind tricks, huh?. Time to call for reinforcements.

'Ma, Pa! You'd best come quick. Mr Fettock says we've won the ...'

I didn't even get to finish the sentence. Ma and Pa belted down the hallway, thrusting me to one side. Bessie and Bugface followed pushing me from behind, trying to see what was going on.

'He's joking, right. I mean we did save the pilp plant from being sold, didn't we? Surely he's just kidding...' said Bugface anxiously.

For the unfamiliar, the pilp plant was where the pilps we collected from donors were ground down to produce energy for the community in exchange for credits which were used as currency. At the same time the sparkle extractor removed the magic dust which changed into metal discs under the pilp donor's pillow.

Bessie gawped in horror, her hands clasping her face. 'Mrs Plishett won it last month. My mum says she's never been the same since.'

'Thanks for that, Bess. I really don't think we need to hear that right now,' I said.

' ... my mum said that she came home one afternoon and they'd burnt all her antique furniture and replaced it with new stuff.'

'You're not really helping, Bess,' I whispered into her face, 'are you?'

'I was just saying ... – ow!' Amazing how a hefty

stamp on the foot can suddenly stop an unwanted conversation!

Victor poked his head through Pa's legs to see what all the fuss was about.

'No, Mr Fettock, we don't want the prize. Give it to the second place winner with our regards,' said Pa. He made a move to close the door again but a large brown shoed foot blocked its closure.

'There is no second place winner, just the first prize.' Mr Fettock's broad smile portrayed a man who was determined to give away the raffle prize no matter what.

Pa wasn't going to give in without a fight though. 'Hasn't this family done enough for the community already?' He pulled me in front of him as his next line of defence. 'Didn't our Aggie stop Arty Granger from getting his hands on the pilp plant and turning us all into Grublins? Surely that counts for something!'

Mr Fettock rose quickly to the challenge. 'Yes, and I can assure you he'll be imprisoned for a long time but ... it's precisely that kind of community spirit that makes you such worthy winners.'

Great! So now it would all be my fault – again!

'I just need a signature for the receipt and then I'll leave you to it.' He held out a pen and a piece of crumpled paper.

'Don't you go signing anything Pa, not least 'til

you've read the small print,' cried Ma.

Pa shook his head despairingly and threw his hands behind his back. Following his lead we all shrunk back from the doorway, thrusting our hands deep into pockets or pushing them far away from the danger of the pen. But from behind Myrtle's leg a small green hand reached out. Victor had already spotted the pen and grabbed it eagerly from Mr Fettock's hand. He began scribbling on the receipt.

'mppl, ju't zpv!' He held it up and thrust it into Myrtle's face proudly.

'No, no, Victor, it's not for drawing on ...' she screamed, frantically grabbing the pen from his sweaty green hand. But it was too late.

'Thank you, that'll do nicely.' Mr Fettock's grin was broader than ever.

'But you can't take that – it's not a signature, it's a scribble!' pleaded Ma.

'Like I said – that'll do nicely. Now for your prize – you have won ...' he paused as if waiting for a drum roll. But we all knew what was coming and dutifully finished the rest of the sentence for him.

'... a month with Stan and Alf Trollit.'

A look of dismay took over our faces as he produced, from behind his back, the six year old, orphaned, Trollit twins. He pushed them towards Ma who took a step backwards trying to avoid the inevitable conclusion to Mr Fettock's visit.

To look at them initially they seemed ordinary little fairies but we all knew there was a much darker side to them. A large thick fringe hid their blue eyes and a mop of blonde hair covered any space available on their heads. The identical green moss jackets and shorts they were wearing did nothing for their shape as both were quite stout, causing them major problems when it came to flying. Well flying, in their case, wasn't really the correct word, perhaps flumping was more closer to the truth. You see, they kind of took off and jumped and bounced a lot. Okay, some flying did occasionally happen in between the jumping and bouncing admittedly. And landing, well that was just pot luck. They seemed to land where they fell.

'Oh come on Mrs Lichen. Look at their dear little faces – well not too closely. Just take their little hands – perhaps not a good idea but they've got gloves on. All they need is a little love and understanding.'

All they needed was locking up behind bars for a very long time. Harsh maybe, but tell that to Mrs Plishett!

'We've got credits, Mr Fettock. How about a few extra for you to re-draw the raffle?' Pa made one last effort.

'No, no, no, Mr Lichen. I'm a government official, no, no, no! The prize has been won and that, I'm afraid, is that. Now, Stan and Alf, say hello to your new family.'

'Hello, new family,' they said quietly in unison. 'Thank you for having us.'

'See, and such polite manners too,' commented Mr Fettock. 'Dear, dear, is that the time? I must dash, important meetings to attend etc. Have fun now.' He turned, spread his wings and without so much as a glance back, flew off in the direction of town.

'Marvellous, bloody, marvellous!' screamed Ma, pushing her way back through the house to the kitchen, 'Raffle prize, huh? How can that be a prize?' She slammed the kettle onto the stove. A very large pot of full strength nettle tea was needed here.

She was followed quickly into the kitchen by Pa who was also ranting and raving.

'What ever happened to prizes that you could spend?' he cried. 'One hundred credits would have come in handy but no, oh no – we get prizes that ...'

'Don't even say it!' she said quickly.

A heavy stomping of feet signalled Myrtle's entrance into both the kitchen and the conversation. 'It's not fair! Why do we have to have them?'

'Why do we have to have what?' said Albert, brushing past Myrtle to get to the rose bread. His skinny body slid easily through the narrow gap between the chair and the kitchen table.

'Where've you been? We've just had a terrible shock and you were nowhere to be found,' cried Ma.

He was always 'nowhere to be found' because he was always 'working on something'.

'I told you that I had to go and see Fred about my new invention. Crikey Ma. I'm fifteen remember. I can look after myself!'

'Well I'm so pleased that you're so responsible because you've got something else to look after now. Aggie, bring them through.'

Albert stared hard at her, desperately begging for an answer. 'Ma, what are you on about?' He ran his hand through his straight jet black hair and frowned deeply.

'Just be patient, dear.'

Being the obedient fairy that I was, and being so grateful that I wasn't the chosen one, I marched off in the direction of the front door which had inadvertently been closed on the raffle prizes. I could hear poor Albert's voice questioning Ma for more details as she slammed pots and pans around the kitchen. A high pitched whining noise could also be heard – Bugface.

I was kind of hoping that I'd be faced with an empty doorstep as I opened the door – but no, there they stood, just as we had left them.

'Hello, Aggie,' they said quietly together.

'Hel …' Damn! They'd almost got me there. I

ushered them into the house and frogmarched them down the hallway.

'Hello, Bessie,' they said quietly together as we passed.

'Hello ...'

'Bessie, what are you doing? Don't talk to them!' I cried.

'Blast! I nearly forgot. Such sneaky creatures.'

Albert had his back to us as we approached the kitchen door. Ma caught my eye.

'Here, Albert.' She gestured to him to turn around. 'Here are your two new brothers!'

His mouth fell open, his eyes gawped and a cold sweat broke out across his forehead.

'Hello, Albert,' they said quietly together.

'Come on, Ma, please. I mean, I'm only fifteen. How can I look after these two at my age?'

'Oh, so now you're *only* fifteen, huh? Don't get your wings in a twist, Albert. We've all got to take responsibility for them ... '

'Hello, Ma,' they said quietly together.

' ... and they will have to share your room until the spare room arrives.'

'When will that be, Pa?' Albert's voice had just a hint of an anxious tremor in it.

'It should be attached by tomorrow ...' said Pa.

'Hello, Pa,' they said quietly together.

'... but don't quote me on it!'

Victor, who had been listening intently to the conversation, was perched high up on the saucepan shelf. He glared down at the twins with his large eyes, watching them carefully as they spoke. As Pa finished speaking they immediately looked up, caught his eye and said quietly together, 'ifmmp, wjdups.'

'ifmmp ... px!' The plastic cup that bounced off his head just managed to stop him from completing the sentence.

'Oops! Sorry, Victor,' I said, having taken just a little pleasure in throwing the cup, 'but you could be affected too.' And, I thought to myself, he could get into enough trouble on his own without any help from Stan and Alf. No, the last thing Victor needed was to enter into conversation with the Trollit twins – the most well-behaved, sickeningly polite and disgustingly helpful fairies in all the land!

# Chapter Two

It was left to Albert to show the twins to their *temporary* accommodation and as he led them reluctantly to his bedroom, he could be heard establishing some firm ground rules.

'No tidying up, no making my bed,' he growled unpleasantly. 'And no waking me up when the alarm rings.' His voice trailed off. The door of his bedroom creaked open slowly and the sound of two stout fairies being shoved through the doorway was obvious for all to hear.

Back in the kitchen Ma and Pa stood glaring at each other. Bugface played it wise and stayed firmly in the hall with me, Bessie and Victor. The staring continued. It moved a step further into scowls and tutting until at last Ma caved in.

'You bought those tickets, didn't you? I told you to stop, not to buy anymore, didn't I? But oh, no ...'

'What are you on about? Why on Mirvellon ...' Pa bit back.

This was in need of some serious interrupting by yours truly.

I cleared my throat noisily, 'Hmm hmm! We're going to head off now ...' I waved my hand around madly, trying to draw attention to myself.

Ma pitched back to Pa, ignoring me completely.

'Oh no, you have to do it all your way, go against what ...'

'... I didn't buy the flipping tickets I told you ...' Pa shouted, raising his eyes to the ceiling.

Okay Aggie, try again! 'Excuse me, Pa but I really think we should be off ...' The wooden spoon, which clipped my ear as it passed through the air, was a clear indication that my words had been disregarded once more.

'... well, don't think I'm cooking for them ...' screamed Ma.

'... you won't have to, *dear* they'll cook for us all – interfering little helpers ...' Pa retorted sourly.

Oh, enough! 'WHEN YOU'VE BOTH QUITE FINISHED!'

Ma glared at me, her lower jaw fell open. Her brow furrowed in anger.

I resumed normal volume and continued in a feeble voice. 'Er, it-it's just that we've got to go now or we'll miss the crossing, okay?' Had I pushed my luck too far? Ma's fearsome look said I had – perhaps I'll be grounded. No such luck. They needed me out collecting tonight!

'She's right,' said Pa. 'They'd better get off or there'll be no pilps left to collect.'

She moved her irate glare from him – to me! 'Well you'd better take the raffle prizes with you!'

I'd better what? Oh, I don't think so. No way.

That's just not gonna happen. Not in this lifetime.

Seeing the look on my face she then added, 'or perhaps you'd like them to stay in *your* room?'

'No, that's perfectly fine. I'll happily take them. Always glad of the extra help!' I said, gritting my teeth hard as I spoke, deflecting her glare. Marvellous, pigging marvellous.

'We'd really better go, Aggie,' Bessie said quietly, tugging at my arm to pull me away from Ma's stare. 'It won't be so bad. There'll be plenty of us to keep an eye on them. Come on, Fred'll wonder where we are.'

Oh great! Wait 'til *he* sees the baggage I've got and this time it isn't just Bugface!

*******

It took sometime to get down to the crossing mainly because the twins kept stopping to let other fairies go past. 'After you,' they said together. Then they stopped to tidy up a tree! Yes, they actually tidied its leaves. And, as we few over Pilpsville, they couldn't resist cleaning one of the huge mirrored panes at the pilp plant. The irate manager Mr Cruet, Gertie's father, shook his fist in the air and shouted, 'That poster was supposed to be there you little busybodies.'

Blissfully unaware of their crime, the twins waved and called back, 'That's okay, Mr Cruet, glad to be of help.'

Stan rolled the poster up and put it in the rucksack on Alf's back and smiled at his brother.

'Will you two stop grinning at each other? We'll never get through the crossing at this rate.' Bessie grabbed hold of Stan's arm and pulled him along. 'Aggie, get the other one or there'll be hell to pay.'

With Victor and Bugface trailing behind us, we finally made it to the crossing with just minutes to spare. Fred was already there with his younger brother, Groaning Gilbert, a whinger of large proportions.

'So the rumours were true, huh? You won the raffle this month and took both first prizes,' he winked, leaning against a shret tree with a smug expression glued to his face. As he spoke his dark hair fell over his eyes and was casually pushed to one side to reveal his handsome features. He was dressed in his usual get up of long trousers and long sleeved tunic, finished off with a broad belt slung over his hips. Draped over his arm was his favourite jacket. He cast a quick eye over me then said, 'What's with the black, huh? Not a death I hope.'

'She's reckons she's a goff!' mumbled Bessie apologetically.

'Oh, right – what's that then?' he asked.

'Not now, Fred!' I answered gruffly. 'Just get the twins away from Gilbert.'

Gilbert, as ever, was clearly not amused about the raffle prize situation. Although, being such a reveller in misery, he had no doubt taken some strange pleasure in our misfortune. His sombre expression, matched by his clothing, gave nothing away though. 'They seem alright to me,' he mumbled as the Trollit twins combed his thick black hair and tried in vain to keep the trademark Trickle crown tuft flat.

'Fine, you keep them,' I said, knowing full well that the prize, once signed or scribbled for, was non-transferable.

The crossing, a portal that lies between the enormous spreading roots of the sacred oak tree, was as busy as ever. One day, I thought, we'll be first in line – but not while we've got so much baggage! As the two suns set behind the Creaganic Hills, the gateway to the other side – the world of humans – revealed itself once more. Fairies from all over Pilpsville piled through. We, of course, were right near the back.

'This is all your fault,' I said, pointing to the twins. 'Why did you have to stop and clean that window?'

'Ah, so that's why you were late,' said Fred. 'What was on the window, a dragonfly splat?'

The twins looked at him in dismay. 'No Fred,' they said together, 'there was an ugly poster breaking the beautiful sheen on the mirrored glass. Look, see for yourself.' Stan pulled the poster out of Alf's rucksack and handed it over to Fred.

'Crikey, Fred, we're late enough. Look at it later,' I said, holding Myrtle's arm as I fly-pushed through the crowds. 'I'd like an early one tonight so we can go to the Juice Bar. Mrs Cheric's doing a special indoor fruit-be-que to mark its tenth anniversary.'

'Right then. What are we waiting for?' called Bessie from behind. With Stan and Alf firmly attached to her hands, she swept past and drove her way through the crowds. Fred shoved Victor out in front like a scary night light. The sight of a sprite was still quite terrifying to those fairies who hadn't encountered one before which made them move just a little quicker. Gilbert, miserable as ever, held tightly on to Fred's arm as they flew.

'I hate speeding,' he groaned as they passed.

********

Our exit from the portal was met with great relief as at last we could begin the nightsgritch in earnest. The weather, however, was not on our side. It was what the humans called winter. Not a nice time to collect pilps at all, especially when the cold wet white stuff arrived.

'It's freezing,' said Bessie, pulling the horrid brown jacket she was wearing around her.

For once I envied her clothing. My thin black

jacket and netted dress were hardly going to keep me warm tonight but at least my matching boots were feather lined.

'Right, we really are going to have to be quick tonight. And remember to keep your wings moving at all times or they'll cease up,' I said, sounding strangely like Ma.

'Who put you in charge?' laughed Fred, buttoning up his blue jacket and turning up the collar. 'Here, Gilbert, you can wear my scarf.' He threw the red woollen strip to his brother. 'It doesn't match your dull clothes but at least it'll keep you warm.'

And quiet, I thought, if he wraps it round his mouth!

'Okay, we'll meet you back here in a couple of hours,' said Fred, grabbing Gilbert by the scarf and fluttering upwards.

'Hold up. Haven't you forgotten something? Where's the cabbage?' I said.

Sheltering in a nearby Always Green tree was Victor. 'j xbju ifsf – upp dpme.' He wrapped some leaves around his tiny body and crawled back to a little nook in the tree trunk.

'One less to worry about,' said Bessie as she prepared for take off.

'Hang on! You can't leave me here with Bugface and the twins.'

'Well, I've got Gilbert,' said Fred, 'and that's

enough for anyfairy to suffer.' He looked at the miserable wretch flapping breathlessly by his side. The miserable wretch mumbled something unintelligible under his breath and gave Fred the evil eye.

We all looked at Bessie. 'What? Surely you don't expect me ... I can't look after both of ...' She folded her arms crossly, 'Oh, alright but don't blame me for any nonsense they get up to.'

'Just keep them close to you. They're not really used to all this, remember,' I said.

'Yeah, I know – show them the ropes and all that.'

'Are we going to look at some ropes, Bessie?' The twins asked in earnest. 'We know lots of good knots like the reef knot, the sheep shank, the double hitch and ...'

'Ah, just come on, will you?' Bessie took each twin by the hand and flew off to the left side of our patch, which just left me and Bugface alone – again. 'We'll head for the big red house with all the windows, right – and no flapstopping please!'

'D'you mean – like this?' Bugface smirked, stopped fluttering her wings and at once dropped through the air like a stone.

'What d'you go and do that for?' I called as I swooped quickly down underneath her.

She screeched to a halt and started flapping again.

'How on earth ...' My mouth dropped open in

astonishment. Flapstopping, literally meaning to stop flapping the wings, had been a major problem where Bugface was concerned. She usually had no control.

'Albert showed me – and he gave me this to try out. He's going to call it the anti-flapstopper.'

Hmmmm, such an original name!

In her hand was a wooden device, circular in shape with a small wire protruding which was touching her hand.

'I squeeze it when I want to stop and a fizz comes out that makes my wings start flapping again.'

'It's not a fizz, you twit, it's an energy shock. You shouldn't let Albert test out his inventions on you.'

'I was just helping out,' she said grumpily as we landed on a nearby window ledge.

'Okay but don't keep doing it – you'll frighten something to death with your hair standing on end like that.' Talk about a bad hair day!

'Must run in the family,' came a snigger from behind a large shret tree. 'I mean look at *her* hair – and she has the cheek to criticise her sister. Well that's rich!'

Just bloody great! Raffle prizes and school bully, Gertie Cruet, all in one day.

I took a deep breath and instigated my first line of defence – a broad smile, the same one that reduced her to a quiver before – but would it work this time?

My heart beat a little quicker as I tried to beat her at her own game. 'Gertie! How *un*pleasant to see you, and I see you've brought the faithful hounds with you too.' Violet and Petunia Millet appeared snarling and spitting from behind a nearby bush fitting my initial description perfectly.

'No need to be like that, Lichen,' she said, then added, 'Oh hell, she's grinning again.'

Smile success once again!

She made a vain attempt to smooth down the frizzy mop of brown hair that possessed her like a demon. Her pointed facial features seemed to be more elongated than usual. 'I really don't know how you put up with *her*, Myrtle. She's such a loser.' She made an 'L' with her fingers and sniggered.

Myrtle grimaced, shying away from the bully and her gang.

'Such a pity – *I'd* have loved a younger sister. You could always join us.' Myrtle blushed and shuffled her feet nervously. Gertie Cruet often had this effect on fairies.

'Oh my portals! Have you seen what she's wearing? Oh dear, has somefairy died?' she said in a faked voice of concern.

'I'm a goff, if you must know. It's fashion ...'

'It's human fashion – that's what it is,' she scoffed. 'Always desperate to be like them aren't you?'

'What *is* it you want, Gertie?' I asked.

She smirked and stared directly at Myrtle. 'Oh, nothing really, just revenge, payback, retribution – call it what you will but I will have it, Lichen – in my own time.' She beckoned to the Millet sisters who flew immediately to her side. 'Anyway, can't stop, dearie – we've got a mystery to solve.'

'A mystery – what mystery?' I said, trying not to sound too intrigued.

'Oh, haven't you heard?' She turned her face to me, complete with a full lip curling sneer and continued, 'It would appear that somefairy's been collecting pilp imitators and they're contaminating the pilp plant energy system. I'm surprised nofairy told you! You being such a sleuth or is it a sluice?' She covered her mouth as if to stifle a giggle.

'I-I-I've been rather busy,' I said, cross with myself for stumbling on my words. 'There's probably a message waiting for me at home.'

'Yeah, right. Like any fairy's going to want you. I mean, you can't even dress properly.' She pointed to me and giggled, 'Loser!' Then with the Milletts tucked in just behind her, she flew upwards, disappearing into the frosty night air.

'It's inside out, Aggie,' whispered Myrtle. 'Your jacket – it's inside out.'

'Bloody Hell! Why didn't you tell me?'

'We were all in such a hurry, you know, what with the twins arriving and all that ...' She looked down guiltily, clutching at her hem before straightening her own jacket. 'S-Sorry, if I'd have known ...'

'Oh save it, Bugface!' I yanked the jacket angrily off my back. 'Perhaps Gertie Cruet *should* adopt you as her sister. You clearly like her more than me!'

'But I said I was sorry ...'

'Just shut it. Not another word,' I said, turning the guilty jacket the correct way.

An angry silence fell between us as I struggled to pull the wretched arms through. Less speed more haste ...

'Aggie.'

'I said no talking.' I thrust my arm crossly through a sleeve.

'But what are pilp imitators?'

'Er doh! Don't you know anything?' I straightened the collar of the jacket before continuing. 'They're what the older humans use when all their own pilps have worn out. You've seen them – in glasses of water by their beds.'

'Oh, those,' she sighed.

'Yeah, those.'

The mood lightened a little as we took off once more for the big house with the red door, swooping low to avoid the bare stiff winter branches that poked through the air like gnarled old granny fingers.

'Brrrr. This cold's going right through me,' Bugface shivered.

'Well speed up, then.' I pushed hard and she followed quickly behind me.

The familiar sight of the tall, many windowed red house, with the toy littered back yard, was a great relief. At least the old crumbling window sills offered some shelter from the seasonal weather with their large overhangs.

'I so love this place,' I said as the pilp detector beeped softly. 'Pilps paradise!'

We landed carefully outside a third floor window, making sure the cracks weren't too wide for us to slip between. A green mossy growth had taken over much of the concrete providing a soft cushion for us to walk on. Inside the lights dimmed giving us the okay to venture in to collect.

But just as we made our move, my sixth sense aerial started twitching.

'Somefairy's trying to get hold of us. Here, hang on to my pilp sack while I try to get a better reception.' I shook an icicle off the end and rubbed the tip between my fingers.

It was Bessie. 'I've got a problem with the Trollits. You need to come now! I'm at the blue house with the wishing well – and hurry.'

Great! With us for five minutes and causing havoc already. I'd have to go and sort them out. Myrtle's face fell as I told her.

'Can't I come with you?' she pleaded.

'No, I told you. I want to get away early tonight so we need all the pilps you can get. Now get a shift on. You've had enough practice.'

'It's not fair. I'm just an apprentice collector.' She stomped sulkily across the length of the window sill causing crumbs of plaster and concrete to throw themselves unwillingly to the ground. 'You're not supposed to leave me,' she added.

'What choice do I have, huh? I can't be in two places at once. Anyway, Albert's bound to be along in a minute.'

'But Aggie ...' she called as I took off for the blue house.

'I'll be quick. Don't worry ...' I shouted back down wind but I wasn't sure if she heard me.

If I quickly picked up the twins from Bessie then I'd be back with Bugface before you could say grumbling Grublins! I pushed my wings hard and before long had the blue house in my sights.

I landed carefully on the window ledge which, apart from a very stroppy Bessie, was completely quiet and bare.

'I told you I couldn't do it,' she protested.

'Why? Where are they?' I asked anxiously, looking around. Losing the raffle prizes wasn't in our best interest.

Bessie pointed at the window. I pushed my face up to the ice cold pane to see inside.

'What the hell are they doing?' I cried.

'They said they can't possibly go home until they've tidied the pilp donor's room.'

'They can't stay there!' I said.

'Oh you've missed the best. Take a closer look at them,' mused Bessie. 'You're not going to believe this bit.'

Oh – my – wings! 'Why are they dressed like squiggles?'

Bessie stifled a giggle.

'It's not funny, Bess. Donor interaction is strictly forbidden, you know that. If they think we really exist, they'll try and track down our world.'

She straightened up her face and nodded. 'I know but I just turned my back once and they'd disappeared. I tried to get them out but the donor saw them and started dressing them up. I couldn't risk it.'

'How on Mirvellon did they wander in there?' I looked in as the pilp donor, sitting up in bed with both twins in her lap, stroked their heads gently.

'I'd been in here earlier for the pilp and they followed me. I brushed against the donor on my way out. It's kind of hot and sweaty – ill I think.'

'That would explain why it's not screaming or trying to trap them. The donor must be delirious – great! We're going to have to sneak in and get them out – somehow.'

Bessie took a deep breath and slid through the gap in the window. I followed, trying hard to think of a rescue plan.

'Keep dead quiet. We can creep up that way.'

'Okay,' whispered Bessie, 'stay right behind me. Make for the chest of drawers.'

We flew as daintily as we could, across the room towards the chest but were spotted be two pairs of eager eyes.

'Hello Bessie. Hello Aggie,' said the twins, delighted as always to see a familiar face.

The donor looked at the Trollits, then back up at me and Bessie.

'More fairwie dowlies to pway wib,' it said, a river of sweat dribbling down its pale little face. Its arm sprang out to grab the two newest additions to the toy box.

'I don't think so!' Bessie dodged the grabbing arm and headed for the window sill.

I landed beside her. 'If I distract it first, you can pull Stan and Alf up and fly them out the window gap.'

'What about you? How will you get out?'

'Haven't thought about that bit. Just get them out and take them to Bugface. She's at the big house with the red door. I shouldn't have left her alone for so long.'

'You'd better do whatever you're going to do now.

I don't like the way it's holding the twins up like that,' said Bessie, nodding towards the donor.

Oh, no! It may be ill but that's going too far …

'Do fairwie dowls bouwnce?' Stan and Alf, AKA the squiggle brothers, hit the floor with such force that they ricochet off the bed and landed with a thump on top of the wardrobe.

CRASH!

'Ouch … er, shall we tidy up the clothes while we're here?' Stan asked Alf shakily.

'Oooh – let me just get my wings straightened out first, then we can set to work,' replied Alf, pressing the nets and bones back into position. Then they disappeared through the wardrobe doors.

It was time to make my move. I swooped down in front of the wardrobe, landing on the door key and peered round the side of the door. 'You two – out now. Can you fly?' I kind of knew the answer to that already – after all they never flew, they flumped!

'Can you give us just two minutes to dust this ledge? This squiggle tail sure comes in handy …' said Alf – or was it Stan?

I reached inside and grabbed whatever felt furry. Two startled squiggle faces appeared, ears first.

'Out now! Make for the window. Bessie will take you back.'

'But …'

Pursing my lips and furrowing my brow did the

trick as the two of them flumped clumsily towards Bessie.

The donor, seeing them exit the wardrobe door, stumbled out of bed landing awkwardly on the floor.

'Come on, Aggie. Make a fly for it,' call whispered Bessie.

'I can't just leave the donor in this state. It looks really pasty!'

'Leave it. We're not supposed to interfere. Now come on,' Bessie called.

'Go, I'll catch you up. I just need to attract the parent donor's attention.'

Bessie shrugged her shoulders and flew off dragging the squiggle twins with her.

If I could only find something to make it cry ... I looked around the room and spotted a small object in a corner. It was just light enough for me to carry. 'Sorry about this,' I said, launching the missile at its unsuspecting target, 'It's for your own good, honestly.'

SMACK!

'Waaaaaahhhh.' It let out an enormous yell which was met by confused voices rushing up the stairs to investigate.

The parent donor rushed into the room and seeing the distressed pilp donor immediately called out for more help.

It needs a cold, wet flannel, I thought. And sure

enough, another parent donor appeared with a cold, wet cloth.

'But the fairwie dowls ...' it clawed frantically at the air but I was already well on my way to the window sill and slid easily through the crack.

With the broad smile of kindness thrust across my face I made my way back to the red house with all the windows. A sense of pride swelled up inside me – I had probably saved that donors life. I was *such* a hero ...

But as the red house came into view, my thoughts of heroism were disturbed by the strange sight of an overcrowded window ledge.

'Why the glum face, Gilbert?' I said sarcastically as I swooped in. He did glum *so* well.

'You'd better take a look at this, Aggie,' called Bessie as I landed. The twins, still disguised as squiggles, flumped around noisily on the ledge beside me.

Fred and Gilbert were standing awkwardly in front of a particular point of the window.

As they parted, I saw my first glimpse of what they'd been hiding.

'It's the ugly poster on the pilp plant window,' said the twins. 'We cleaned it up, we did!'

Fred reached into his back pocket and pulled out the poster he'd been given by Stan. He shook his head in disbelief and slumped down on the red house window ledge.

'Take a closer look,' ushered Bessie, her hands trembled as she pointed to the window.

It was a crudely drawn wanted poster for an escaped prisoner.

'What's this got to do with me?'

'The picture, Aggie – it's him! He's out.'

I tore frantically at the tatty paper, pulling it off the window pane in two pieces. 'How can he be out? He's confined to Mursham Marshes. He got 12 months.'

'He may well have but he's escaped … and that's not the worst of it.' Bessie looked around to Fred for support but his head, cradled in his arms, was hung low.

'Never mind him! Where's Bugface? I told you to meet her here, Bess. Where is she?'

'L-L-Look at the bottom of the poster, Aggie!' She draped her arm around my shoulder. 'He got to her first. She's been kidnapped – by Arty Granger!'

# Chapter Three

'Why did you leave her on her own, Aggie?' cried Ma, burying her head in her apron.

'I told you, I had to go and fetch the twins,' I said quietly. 'They were interacting with a donor, Ma. I had to go and help Bessie get them out.'

'But your own sister – your little sister – you shouldn't have left her alone,' Ma lifted her head briefly, let out a choking cry then covered her face once more with the red checked material of her apron.

Pa leant across the table and moved a cup of soothing nettle tea towards her. 'Here dear, try some of this. The twins made it especially ...'

'Why those little ...' She leapt out of the kitchen chair and threw herself towards the cooker where Stan and Alf stood nervously.

Pa grabbed her before she could do much harm but from the look on their faces the twins hadn't encountered such rage before. 'No Ma, this isn't the twins fault.'

' ... but if they hadn't ...'

' ... then he'd have found another way of getting her – or indeed Aggie, seeing as she seems to be the target of his revenge, if this note is anything to go by!' Pa pushed the note firmly in front of Ma's mournful face, tapping it with his fingers as he spoke.

'You read it, Pa. I can't bear to see his evil writing.' She sat up and wiped her sodden eyes for what appeared to be the millionth time that evening.

Pa held the note at arms length, cleared his throat and read the words out loud. ' "Well, Lichen, looks like I've had the last laugh after all. Don't tell anyfairy about this or the Bugface will get it. I'll be in touch!" '

'That's it? I'll be in touch?' said Ma in despair.

'How the hell did he escape? I thought his wings were supposed to have been clipped,' said Albert, then distracted by the curious sight of the twins, added, 'and why are the twins dressed as squiggles?'

'Perhaps if you'd have been out with us you'd know the answer to that,' I said bitterly.

'I was busy working on ...'

'Anti-flapstoppers, yeah! You should have been there, Albert, but you're always too busy ...'

*BANG!* The loud crash of the front door surprised everyfairy except Pa.

'That'll be Ferrett. I sent a dragonfly message as soon as I knew. He'll have some answers, hopefully.' Pa looked down the hallway and called, 'Come in Ferrett, the door's open.'

'But Pa, it said ...' cried Ma.

'Yes, I know but I had to do something, besides, Ferrett's alright – he won't say a thing.'

Ferrett Granger was a close family friend – he was also Arty's uncle. Although known to be mean with his credits, he was always on hand to help in a crisis. Especially seeing as most of them involved his own *sweet* nephew!

As he entered the room he took a deep breath and gasped. 'Oh no! I take it it's very bad news.' He looked from me to Pa.

'Sorry?' said Pa not fully understanding Ferrett's comments. 'Oh, no – that's just Aggie's new human fashion. She's a cough!'

'A goff, Pa!' I said, realising that at this time my black clothing could cause confusion.

'I'm so sorry about all this,' said Ferrett striding towards the table. His height and physique portrayed a man of wealth and importance. 'I really thought we'd put an end to all his antics!'

Pa raised his eyebrows then slid the kidnap note across the table to Ferrett.

'Hmmm,' Ferrett stroked his long grey beard thoughtfully as he read through the words. 'Judging by the state of this handwriting, his mind seems to have gone. All that time in solitary confinement must have taken its toll.'

'He could do anything!' said Albert.

'He's one desperate fairy,' said Ferrett.

'We could get up a crowd and storm Mursham Marshes.' Albert pounded his fist in his hand angrily.

'No!' Ferrett had other ideas. 'I think it may be wiser to keep this to ourselves besides, we can't get near the marshes at the moment. A thick putrid fog seems to have encompassed the whole island. It's been blown across from Grublin City. It could be weeks before we can land.'

'But my poor Myrtle.'

'Try to be brave, Mrs Lichen,' said Ferrett in a low, comforting voice. 'If Arty's got her there, it's just a matter of time before you get her back. Meanwhile, I suggest you all go about your business as usual.'

'What about school?' said Ma, trying hard to compose herself.

'Make up an excuse,' said Ferrett

'Wing rot!' I said loudly.

'I beg your portal!' said Ferrett indignantly.

'We can tell the school she's got wing rot. It'll keep them all well away seeing as it's so contagious.' I was amazed at my own ingenuity but was quickly brought down by Ferrett.

'Good idea! And then you can set about tracking down your sister, yes?'

Then I could what? Astounded, I looked up at him and then at Pa. 'I'm sorry?'

'Look – how can I fly such a distance?' Pa turned and angrily flapped his shrivelled wing. 'Don't you think I'd rather go myself than send you?' He clapped his hands to his face.

'Now, now Pa,' said Ma taking over the reassuring role.

'Well you're the obvious choice, Aggie. You tracked him down before ...' Ferrett tilted his head in what was meant to be a persuasive pose then raised his eyebrows to add to the effect.

'No, I was looking for Albert because I thought he was *the light*. You know the one that was helping Arty to buy the pilp plant, didn't it Albert?' I looked to him for support but he shrugged his shoulders.

'Ferrett's right, Aggie,' he shuffled his feet uncomfortably. 'You know the way Arty works much better than any of us – I'll help where I can.' He looked up at me. I've got some great inventions underway ...'

'Well, that's big of you seeing as she's your sister too!' Bloody hell! Just because I'd saved all the pilp collectors on Mirvellon, I was deemed the chosen one! Hmmm, the chosen one – it had a good ring to it. Ah, just one tiny problem! 'But Arty hates me,' I cried. 'He'll kill me for half a truffnut!'

'That's my point, dear. You're very close to him. Though I think *kill* is rather a strong word to use,' said Ferrett. He looked across at Pa, willing him to speak. Pa obliged.

'And somefairy needs to look after Ma,' he said, squeezing Ma fondly. 'And Albert, well, he'll have to take on the majority of pilp collecting.'

I couldn't help but snigger inwardly at that point. Albert Lichen; pilp collector! What a joke. We'd all starve to death if he was in charge.

'It's a lot to ask, Aggie, I realise that but who else can we turn to?' Ma wrung out the corner of her apron as she spoke, causing little beads of tear water to form and dribble down over her knees. 'You know what that poster said ...' she added.

'Yes,' I said, 'I know what it said. Don't worry Ma, I'll find her.' I wasn't sure how or even where but I had to try.

*BANG!* Another loud crash as the door hit the wall and interrupted what should have been a family moment. The sound of thumping footsteps running down the hallway filled our ears.

'Ooops, sorry to barge in,' puffed Bessie breathlessly. 'I did knock but the door was open.' Her hair, originally two neatish brown plaits, resembled a rather large bird's nest now which she swept back away from her eyes.

'This really isn't a good time, Bessie,' said Pa, ushering her backwards towards the front door again. 'We were all just going to bed. A clear head is what's needed in times like these.'

'But I couldn't sleep and besides, I found this on the gate.' She held a crumpled yellowy piece of paper aloft. 'It's about Myrtle,' she added softly.

Pa snatched the note hastily from her hand and fell back onto the kitchen chair next to Ma. It rattled noisily on the enamel floor tiles.

'Oh, no. Dear, dear, dear.' He sighed deeply as he read it through.

'Well. What's it say? What's it say?' Ma leant over and grabbed the note from Pa, 'Oh, give it here. I'll read it myself!' Her head moved from side to side as she sucked in the contents of the note. She clasped one hand dramatically to her chest, looked up at the off-white enamel ceiling and let out a huge wail. The paper slipped casually out of her hand and floated under the kitchen table.

'What kind of fairy would do this to an innocent fairychid?' She held up a clump of wiry red hair which had been attached to the paper – it was Myrtle's!

As Pa leant in to comfort her, Ferrett fished around under the table to where the note had landed.

'Let's have a look at his demands then,' he said. 'Hmmm – a ransom of 100 credits and a FFP.'

'A what?' said Pa, lifting his head away from Ma's.

'You know, a Fast Flying Pack – like the one Phyllis Router has,' I chipped in.

'Surely she hasn't still got it. After working in league with Arty …,' said Pa.

'She was a victim too, Pa. She didn't know his plans for all of us,' I added quickly.

Albert grabbed the note from Ferrett, '100 credits? That's a strange amount to ask for. Now 1000 or 10,000 I could understand but just 100 – that just seems – a little odd!' He scratched his chinfluff thoughtfully.

'Shouldn't we be grateful it's such a small amount?' said Pa, snatching the note back. 'At least we have half a chance of finding that amount of credits.'

'Albert's right though, Pa. Can we be sure it's Arty? After all, it does seem rather a small amount to ask for as a ransom,' I said. I caught Albert's eye and nodded to him in agreement.

'Stop! There's no way that anyfairy's paying a ransom, whatever the price, to that nasty excuse for a pilp collector as long as I'm around!' shouted Ferrett. 'If we sent Aggie off now, we should have Myrtle back safely before you can say …'

'Er, send Aggie off to where? Grumbling Grublins. Oh, no, no.' I lowered my voice, aware of the dreadful wheezing noise coming from Bessie's direction. 'You're kidding, right? Grublin City?'

'No need to panic – he's not going to go back there for a while. No, I was thinking more to the south of Pilpsville …' Ferrett paused expectantly and looked directly into my eyes.

South of Pilpsville, huh? Grublins to the north, Pershats to the west, sprites to the …

'What? You want me to go to Spercham – where the sprites live!' It was my turn to gasp and hold my chest.

'Why on Mirvellon would he take her to Spercham?' said Pa, completely ignoring me.

'Well, we know he's been there before. Remember the grey bottles. He got the sprites to make up that 'turning into Grublin' mixture,' chipped in Albert.

'But he wouldn't go back there,' said Ma.

'It's a perfect place to hide. No pilp collector has ever been there or would ever want to go there!' said Ferrett.

'EXCUSE ME!' I retook my position of hand clutched to chest before continuing. 'You want ME to go to Spercham to look for Myrtle. Has it escaped you that I'm not actually, in any way, sprite looking?'

'Well, yes ... but if we use one of those costumes we keep for WitchWatch week,' said Ferrett.

'Yes, there should be one in the old store. Probably needs a little adjustment though,' added Ma.

'You're serious, aren't you? You really think the sprites won't recognise me inside some grotty green costume. And what about the voice – I don't speak spritespiel, ask Victor, he knows.' I poked Victor in the back making him jump sideways and fall into a nearby chair.

'tuvqje gbjsz dbo pomz kvtu tqfbl pxo mbohvbhf. tupq ubmljoh. hp gjoe nzsumf,' he said picking himself up.

'What's he say?' said Pa.

'Exactly my point! None of us understands or speaks spritespiel – ESPECIALLY ME!' I folded my arms crossly. I was all for rescuing Myrtle, after all, I was already a fully qualified heroine, but becoming a sprite – that was a creature too far.

'Ah,' said Albert pushing past me. 'I might have something that could help.' He ran down the hall to his bedroom, throwing the door back noisily. After a few minutes he came rushing back clutching an old cardboard box filled with bits of wire, plastic tubes and various other oddments. He reached in and pulled out a long strip of wide black elastic with a circular piece of plastic stuck firmly in the middle. 'It's a translator. It translates spritespiel into pilp talk and vice versa.'

Oh great! Just what I *always* wanted!

'Here, try it on.' He pushed the contraption in my face. 'Place the plastic piece over your mouth. I'll fasten the elastic at the back.'

'cmppez ifmm, op offe up qvmm ju tp ujhiu!' I screamed.

'Oh my,' cried Ma, 'Aggie's speaking spritespiel!'

'biiiiiii,' shrieked Victor, holding his hands over his ears, 'cbe gbjsz tqfbljoh tqsjuf ubml, biiii!' He ran under the kitchen table and curled up into a small green ball.

'What'd he say, Aggie?' said Albert, excitedly tugging at my arm.

'ipx uif cmppez ifmm ep j lopx? j'wf pomz hpu uif npvuiqjfdf zpv jejpu!'

'Do you want to try the earpiece now?' He said, completely oblivious to what I'd just said. He clipped two small circular pieces of plastic to the sides of my ears and plugged a wire into the back of the mouthpiece. What followed was a frenzy of arm waving and shouting as the earpiece was put through its paces. Unfortunately, the only real way of testing it was with Victor but he was having none of it. He remained tucked up, ball shaped, under the table. I crawled under the table, leant over him and said in a gentle voice, 'xibu't hsffo, spvoe boe sfbmmz tnfmmz?'

The head unfolded itself slowly and two large eyes stared straight into mine. 'mppl jo njssps – uifo zpv gjoe pvu!' With that he bolted under the nearest chair legs on all fours and headed for the kitchen door.

'Xiz zpv …' I screamed after him.

'Right, I think we can safely say that it works. Well done, Albert,' said Ferrett, wrenching the contraption, and some of my hair, from my head.

'Okay,' said Ma. 'Aggie, you'd better head over to the storeroom. It's dark enough for you not to attract too much attention.'

'I'll help – no school tomorrow, remember? It's

Ivor day,' said Bessie. Ivor the Zealous was a champion pilp collector whose statue stood outside the community school. Normally this announcement would lead into a string of dreadful Ivor jokes but this really was no time for laughter.

I grabbed my jacket quickly from the bedroom before returning to the hall where Bessie was waiting.

'Bess, I'm not sure that this imitating a sprite lark is such a good idea. Couldn't we just send Victor to find out if Myrtle's there?'

'Oh come on, you're not scared are you? Aggie Lichen, who saved the whole of Pilpsville from being turned into Grublins.'

'It's not that, well it is a bit – it's just that I could be looking somewhere else while Victor was in Spercham.'

Victor poked his head round the kitchen door. He'd been listening intently to the conversation. 'op, op, op! wjdups opu hpjoh up tqfsdibn po ijt pxo. zpv bmm dpnf xjui nf!'

'What's he say?' said Bessie, her head cocked to one side.

'Like I know – look no translator.' I pointed to my head crossly.

'No need to be rude and grumpy – just 'cos you're going to be a giant cabbage.' She ran down to the front door. 'Come on,' she yelled, 'down to the store room and find that costume. Then let's get your sister back.'

I chased down the hall after her and shouted goodbye to anyone listening, slamming the door behind me.

********

The store room was located at the far end of Pilpsville Major, the senior school. We kept many costumes there from plays and celebrations.

Bessie flung open the door noisily.

'I thought this was supposed to be a secret,' I said, holding my finger to my lip.

'Oh yeah, sorry.' She pushed the door quietly back into place as we stepped through the door. 'Look through that lot on the rail.'

The metal hangers crashed together as we rummaged. 'Oh, look Bess. Here's the one I wore when I played a human in last year's school play.'

'Hmmm, let's not go down that road again, please,' said Bessie, holding up a badly made dragonfly costume.

'The costume your granma made for you. Blimey, I didn't think they'd keep that – no offence meant.'

'None taken, Aggie. After all, it did look pretty awful.'

After a few minutes searching I was ready to give up and go. 'Nothing here, Bess. Let's get out of here.

– 50 –

It's a stupid plan anyway.'

'Not so fast! I know it's here somewhere.' She poked around in the last tatty box on the floor. 'Ah, here it is.' She held up a well worn insipid green piece of cloth that at some time would have passed for a costume.

'You don't seriously expect me to wear that, do you?' I said, kicking the threadbare item to the other side of the room. It threw up a small cloud of dust as it hit the wall.

'Well, what else can you use? Do you see any instant sprite disguises in here?' She marched across and snatched the pile of green crumpled cloth up from the floor. 'Here, try it on.' The suit landed in a heap just by my feet. I looked at it indignantly.

'What here? Right now?' I protested.

'Try it on, now – I'll do you up at the back,' she insisted.

Undressing quickly, I stepped inside and pushed my wings through the two slots at the back, then adjusted the gloves and boots so that all my tooth fairy features were completely covered.

'It's quite authentic looking, really,' said Bessie, attaching the head to the body.

'The only thing authentic about this costume, Bess, is the smell! Phew – it stinks. Get me out of it, quick.'

'Mmmm, seems to be a slight problem,' she said.

'Not a good time to joke, Bess. Get me out,' I yelled.

'I can't – the fastener's stuck.' She stood in front of me and did some odd actions with her hands. 'Try pushing the head off yourself.'

'It won't budge. What am I going to do now?'

*******

'You mean you had to fly all the way home like this?' said Pa, finally wrenching the head part of the costume away from the rest. 'You poor thing.'

I took a large gulp of clean air.

'No fairy saw you, did they?' said Ma, 'There'll be panic if the whole of Pilpsville knows what's happened.'

'No, we kept to the shadows so as not to be seen.'

'Well, you've certainly given young Victor a terrible fright,' said Pa, pointing to the green quivering wreck hiding behind the door.

'At least we know it works,' said Bessie.

'Just be careful with this head. I'm afraid I've weakened the seam where I've pulled it off. It could fall apart at any time,' said Pa. 'I'll stick a piece of gummy tape over the seam just in case. Try it on again, see if it's strong enough ...'

Ma interrupted quickly and took the head piece from his arms, placing it gently on the table. 'No, Pa, no more tonight. Aggie's got a hard day tomorrow. She needs some rest.'

Ma was right. I was completely exhausted.

As the door closed quietly behind Ferrett and Bessie, I settled down to sleep but not before casting a sorrowful look across to the empty bed where Myrtle should have been sleeping.

'Oh, Bugface,' I whispered into the night air, 'Where are you?'

*******

After a fitful night spent tossing and turning, I finally emerged into an eerily silent kitchen just after sunrise. The twins and Albert were still in bed. Ma was sat at the table, hunched over a steaming hot cup of nettle tea while Pa stood at the cooker absentmindedly stirring an empty saucepan with a wooden spoon. It was gloomsville, big time!

Knock, knock!

'Who on Mirvellon can that be at this time in the morning?' I said, hoping for a response as the silence of the kitchen competed against slurps of tea and the faint scraping of wood on metal. 'I'll go and see, yeah?' Still nothing. Sadness and anxiety filled the room and engulfed me like a cold blanket.

I shuffled miserably towards the front door, raking my hand through my unkempt hair and rubbed my face in an effort to look at least half awake. Wrenching the door open with my sleep starved body took all my strength.

'Yes!' I said, abruptly.

'Bloody hell! Don't look now Gilbert but a scary faced monster seems to have taken over Aggie's body. AArrgghh!'

'Oh, very funny, Fred. I'll have you know I've hardly slept a blink and I have a very important mission to complete – and what's more, it's a *secret* mission.' I took a deep breath as the final flurry of words left my lips.

Fred feigned a gasp and held his hands up in a mock expression of surprise. 'You mean the secret mission that involves you dressing up as a sprite and going to Spercham to try and find Myrtle?'

'This is no time for your teasing, Fred Trickle,' I glanced both ways, checking for any eavesdroppers, 'You'd best come in – him too!' I pointed to Gilbert who was hovering around with a large brown rucksack on his back.

'Why do I always have to carry the heavy stuff?' he groaned as he passed through the door way.

'Just take it through to Aggie's Ma and Pa.' Fred raised his eyes to the sky. 'Go on, they'll know what to do.'

With a little more groaning and grunting, Gilbert came to the kitchen where he set the bulging rucksack down noisily on the kitchen table.

The sight of visitors stirred Ma, at last, from her painful thoughts and Pa relinquished his hold on the wooden spoon. They seemed genuinely pleased to see the Trickle brothers.

Fred pushed the rucksack across the table near to where Pa was standing. 'Mum said they're very old and therefore slightly delicate but should serve the purpose.'

Pa grabbed at the bag gratefully and began to unbuckle the strap. 'And your mum's okay about this, huh?'

Fred raised his eyebrows and nodded his head.

'How about you, Fred?' Pa continued, 'Are you sure you're up for it?'

'Up for what?' I said.

'We're going with you – to Spercham. Aren't we, Gilbert?' said Fred, slapping his brother heartily across the back.

Gilbert slumped into a chair and rested his head in his hands sulkily. 'I'm only going because it's Myrtle – if it was you or Aggie …'

'Oh, shut up whinging, please,' said Fred.

Pa tipped the crumpled contents of the rucksack onto the table. 'Look, they've even got their own outfits.' He held up a very tatty looking, sickly green costume complete with head and complimentary stench.

'Oh – my – wings, Fred! You're really going to wear that – for me?' I felt flattered that he thought that much of me as he hadn't shown a great deal of interest since the pilpblast.

'For you? No, Aggie – for Myrtle, remember?' He grinned wickedly.

Back down to Mirvellon with a bump!

# Chapter Four

We wanted to leave for Spercham Forest immediately but Ma and Pa insisted we waited.

'It's far too risky. You'll leave later,' said Ma, tearfully. 'You need to be prepared.'

So the rest of the long day was spent packing and making ready for the hazardous journey. To make matters easier, the translator equipment was packed tightly into a small rucksack. The bulky green sprite costume was pushed and shoved into another bag along with a torch and some reviving mint biscuits to give to Myrtle when we found her.

The plan was to leave for Spercham Forest just before dusk, under cover of darkness. Cabbage breath would lead us to a point just outside the impenetrable barrier where we could change into our costumes. Ferrett's appeal to the healers, who lived high up in the extensive branches of the sacred oak tree, had worked and after much deliberation, they had kindly agreed to allow us to use the barrier piercer. Hopefully we could then slip un-noticed into the land of the sprites to look for Myrtle.

'Best get your head down for a bit,' said Pa, ushering me towards the bedroom. I managed to have a quick nap but all moments of sleep were penetrated with nightmare glimpses of what could lay ahead in Spercham – and fears of what the sprites might have done to Myrtle. I woke with a start.

After a quick slice of rose bread toast I was off leaving Ma and Pa in tears at the prospect of losing another daughter.

'I'll be fine, honestly. Try not to worry,' I said bravely. I choked back a few tears then flew on to Bessie's.

The house seemed strangely quite when I arrived. Just a tiny chink of light shone out from the kitchen window. All around was silent apart from a faint snoring sound coming from a small door situated in the centre of the front door.

'Wadja want?' said the door gnome grumpily as I knocked on his door. His bright blue face had crease lines down one side from where he'd been sleeping.

'Bessie's expecting me,' I said

'At dis time a day?' he grumbled.

'Oh, just tell her I'm here!' Bloody door gnomes – how I hated them. They made the simple task of knocking on a door such a hard one.

The front door suddenly swung open and Bessie's mum appeared.

'Hello, Aggie. Take no notice of Boris, he's just not an early evening gnome are you dear?' She put her hand out to touch the door gnome's bulbous head and found his little door slammed on her fingers.

'Ouch! You little sod!' She blew quickly on her hand and gestured me in with the other. 'I'm not sure I approve of this expedition but I know that if it was Bessie missing you'd be there for her. She's just packing her stuff.'

Before long, Bessie was ready and after a lengthy goodbye to her mum we were off.

'Take care, love,' her mum cried after us. 'I've put your costume in the zip compartment of your bag.'

'You've got a costume? I thought you were going to be on guard outside the barrier,' I said as we soared upwards.

She ignored my comments bringing the conversation swiftly back round to her costume. 'I'm afraid my granma made it! Don't worry, she's sworn to secrecy,' said Bessie, crossing her finger across her heart.

'I'm more worried about the state of the costume. I've seen your granma's handiwork!' I looked over at her as we passed over the grounds of Pilpsville Major where the proud statue of Ivor the Zealous, champion pilp collector stood. 'We've got to be really convincing, Bess. Those sprites won't give us half a chance if they suspect us.'

'I'm sure it's fine,' said Bessie, casting her eyes away suspiciously. 'Anyway, what's happening with the others?'

'Victor's gone to get Fred and Gilbert. We're

meeting them at the back of the pilp plant,' I said. 'It'll be dusk soon and we desperately need the dark if we're to have any chance of getting into Spercham Forest without being noticed.'

We flew swiftly through the town, circling overhead until we saw Fred and Gilbert arrive at the pilp plant with Victor ... and the twins!

'What the bloody hell are they doing here? They'll hold us up!' I said landing gently beside Fred.

'Don't blame us!' groaned Gilbert, twisting the edge of his sleeve. 'Your mum made Victor bring them along. She thought they might be useful.'

'But they've got no costumes. Oh hell, this is going to be a disaster. I can feel it in my wings.' I held my hands up to my head in desperation.

'Hey, it's not so bad,' said Fred, patting my back in a comforting manner. 'They can guard the gap in the barrier when we've gone through.'

'Yeah, I suppose you're right.' I said, 'Come on. We'd best get going – it'll be dusk soon.'

As one complete unit we took to the sky and headed back across Pilpsville, towards the south of the town where the forest of Spercham lay waiting.

*******

We sat huddled together directly beside the impenetrable barrier built so many years ago to keep the screeching sprites out of our land and away from our magic dust. Yet here we were, armed with a barrier piercer and supergloo sealer about to deliberately put the whole of Pilpsville at risk to save the life of one little pilp collector – my sister Myrtle.

Sitting there, hardly daring to talk, I looked around trying to gauge the general feeling. Victor seemed to be the most nervous of all. His whole body shook violently. Every now and then he held on tightly to his stomach then sucked in great lungfuls of air.

'What's the matter with him?' I said as he disappeared for the fifth time behind a tree.

'He's nervous, of course. I mean, he hasn't seen another sprite for ages,' said Gilbert protectively.

Perhaps Gilbert was right but Victor's reactions seemed completely over the top to me. I just couldn't understand why he was so anxious to return to his homeland – and at least he looked like a sprite!

As dusk fell our conversation grew weaker and silence filled the air as the reality of what we had to do sunk in. We couldn't wait any longer.

'It's time,' I said.

We quietly changed into our costumes, leaving the head pieces until last. The twins tidied our clothes away and hid them behind a nearby shret tree. As expected, Bessie's granma had created a sprite outfit that defied all definition. The head piece at least resembled a sprite but the costume itself was a pale green, tight fitting, sparkly disaster.

'Crikey Bess, it's got three arms,' I said, 'and she's sewn green sequins all around the waist. They'll suss you out instantly.'

'Quick Gilbert, give me a hand to pull them off.' Bessie said despondently. 'Fred, you pull the third sleeve back inside the costume.'

'Why do I have to help? I never sewed them on!' Gilbert stamped his feet sulkily.

'We're in this together, remember?' said Fred, crossly. 'For Myrtle ...'

'Alright. Alright. You don't have to keep on!' Gilbert started yanking the sequins off in handfuls.

'Hey, not so rough! You'll rip the costume ...'

Too late!

RIIIPPP!

Clutching the piece of sequined material in his hand, Gilbert stared in disbelief at Bessie's bottom, 'I told you I didn't want to help, didn't I?'

'Oh, you stupid idiot!' cried Bessie holding her hand over the offending area. 'Now what am I supposed to do?'

'Bloody hell!' I threw my hands up in the air in frustration. 'We haven't got time for all this. We need to cut through the barrier.'

Bessie looked at me somewhat forlornly 'But what about my ...'

'Oh, just keep your hand on it! Pass me the piercer – now!'

'Alright! No need to snap,' said Bessie.

Snatching the precious piercer out of her hand, I knelt down and set to work. Well somefairy had to make a move! Within minutes a large but badly gorged hole appeared in the 'impenetrable' barrier, just big enough for us all to crawl through. Warm air rushed through and a strong smell of grass invaded the privacy of our nostrils. Darkness clung to the world of sprites at this time, just as it did ours. The tingle dancing on my spine reminded me of the dangers ahead while the beat of my heart brought my thoughts back to the reasons behind this – Myrtle.

I stood up quickly and wiped my sweaty brow. 'Right, who's first?' A stony wall of silence met my question. A row of sour faced fairies – and a sprite – met my glance as I turned round.

'What?' I said, pushing the piercer back into the bag.

'Sometimes you can be so bossy,' said Bessie, pursing her lips – always a sign that she was not best pleased.

'Well, sometimes I have to be and anyways, it's called being assertive! – So back to the question,' I said, being ever so slightly assertive again!

Fred stood directly behind me. 'Well, somefairy's gonna have to go first.' I felt his hands fall heavily on my shoulders, 'Perhaps it should be ... you!' And with a hefty push it *was* me!

After prising my face out of a large clump of grass, I realised that I'd landed in some kind of clearing. I brought myself up to my knees and had a quick look around. So many trees and so tall. In between each one swirled a green sparkly mist, caressing each branch affectionately and whistling, as if talking to them, as it passed. While the air hung like a huge damp cloth, both humid and heavy.

'So, are we coming through or what?' Fred call-whispered.

'Too right you are,' I gripped Fred's costume tightly and yanked him through the hole. He landed in a messy heap beside me. Far from looking cross he just laughed and brushed himself down. The others followed quickly.

For a few moments we just sat and stared, except for Victor. He paced back and forth, rubbing his hands together anxiously.

'Keep him still, Gilbert,' I said, then added, 'Let's keep moving. This clearing makes us all ideal targets.'

'There's a bushy bit over there.' Bessie pointed to an area about 200 metres away which would serve as a hiding place until we decided on a way forward.

Stealthily, we flew low, landing quietly amongst the selected greenery as intended. It was time for me to make the final transformation.

'Pass me the translator. It's in the bag,' I said in a commanding voice.

Gilbert looked around desperately. 'What bag?'

'Er doh! The bag on your back! The bag I gave you outside the barrier!'

Gilbert felt tentatively behind him, 'I don't have it,' he said, rubbing his head in a confused manner. 'I did have it – but I don't now.'

'We hung it up for you,' said the twins in unison.

'Great – so let's have it,' I said, holding out my free hand, my patience waning by the minute.

'Okay, we'll set off straight away.' With that, they flapped their squatty wings together frantically as they prepared to take off.

'Oi!' I said, grabbing Alf's right leg before he had the chance to fly. 'Where the hell have you left it? Hang about, why are you two still here? We left you on guard outside the barrier.'

'We sealed the gap so that the sprites can't get out,' they began, 'and we tidied everything out of sight, hung up inside the trees.'

'Yes, yes, yes, that's very good of you but you were supposed to be there for when we returned. You know, to re-open the gap with the barrier piercer ...' I stalled, realising that when the twins meant tidy every thing they meant – oh, no! I stretched my arms out straight and flexed my fingers. 'Please don't tell me you tidied everything away – not all the bags.'

'Well,' said Stan, 'we couldn't leave things laying around for other fairies to see, could we? They might get suspicious.' Alf nodded in agreement. 'All the bags are hidden away safely inside the blue shret tree.' They looked at each other and smiled proudly. 'All clean and tidy,' they said together.

'You fools! Those bags had the translator and the barrier piercer in them!'

'Oh, marvellous. How the hell are we going to get back?' cried Bessie.

'More to the point, how are we going to find Myrtle without the translator?' said Gilbert, flopping down to the floor clutching his head.

'Op!' said Victor firmly, slapping at Gilbert's hand as he absentmindedly made a move to dislodge his headpiece. 'nvtu opu ublf pgg zfu, hjmcfsu.'

Fred, clearly amused by the spread of assertiveness, grinned and said 'Looks like that's where you come in, little brother … you and your green mate!' He put his hand on Gilbert's shoulder. 'You'll have to use what spritespiel you know to get us through this.'

'Oh, what? Why's it always me that gets to do all the grotty jobs? It's not fair.' He shrugged Fred's hand away and threw his arms into his speciality crossed and sulky arrangement. His little eyes peered angrily, with the help of the thick black glasses, from inside the insipid green head piece.

'We can help ...,' Alf began.

'I think you've helped us enough, don't you?' said Bessie bitterly.

'But we ...,' implored Stan, stretching out his hands.

'No more! Just be quiet while we figure things out.' Bessie gestured and obediently the twins sunk slowly to the floor.

'Well there's no way we can leave them here,' I said quickly.

'But they've got no costumes', said Bessie.

'Er doh! Don't you think I know that?' I retorted sarcastically.

'We need something green – some green dye or ..., said Fred

'...or green ink,' Bessie said excitedly.

'...or Victor could just throw up all over them,' said Gilbert in his usual droll manner. 'It's always green when he's sick,' he added informatively.

'Or we could just watch as the twins turn themselves green,' I said not actually believing what I was seeing. I blinked then wiped my eyes before fixing my glare once more upon them. As they sat face to face with each other, Alf and Stan pressed the palms of their hands together and a river of green flowed across their skin right to the roots of their hair. Once completely green their wings grew longer and lighter and their faces contorted as they slowly took on the inimitable features of Spercham sprites.

'Bloody Hell!' Bessie cried but her voice was quickly muffled by Fred's hand across her mouth. He put a finger on his lips to gesture silence. 'Sorry, Fred,' she whispered, 'I've never seen that happen before.' She blushed a little and lowered her eyes.

'How can you do that?' groaned Gilbert. 'It's impossible! It's not fair. Why can't I do that, Fred?'

'Because,' his brother whispered, also clearly fascinated by what he was witnessing, 'they're Metamorphs – changelings. They can morph into other creatures at will.'

The minutes ticked by as we all stood watching, mouths wide open, as the final transformation took place. As the last strand of hair retreated back into their scalps and the width of their mouths extended into the correct position, they were ready.

I broke the silence, 'Yeah, great – okay, show's over. Victor, you'd better lead ...'

'bbbbbbbbiiiiiiii.' The nearby trees trembled as together the twins emitted a loud ear piercing scream.

Now I was really angry. They'd put the whole mission at risk. 'What the hell did you go and do that for?'

'We had to practise our blood curdling screams otherwise those sprites over there will wonder what we're all doing.' They pointed to one of the smaller trees just beyond the clearing we'd just left, where a group of youth sprites had just arrived and were huddled together among the widespread branches.

Victor clasped a small green hand to his head. 'pi, op. ju't opscfsu boe ijt hboh.' Hiding behind Gilbert's legs, he watched nervously as the gang descended from their secret tree house and crept towards us.

'What'll we do?' Bessie said. The panic in her voice apparent as it wobbled anxiously reflecting all our thoughts.

'tdsfbn,' whispered Victor, straining his head round Gilbert's kneecap. 'tdsfbn mjlf ifmm. uifo fmefst xjmm dpnf.'

Gilbert translated quickly.

'Hold on – surely the last thing we want is for more sprites to come,' said Bessie.

'Yeah, Bessie's right. We can sort out these sprites ourselves!' said Fred.

'cfuufs cf dbvhiu cz fmefst uibo cz opscfsu!' said Victor.

'I really think we should trust Victor,' said Gilbert. 'He'll make sure we don't get found out. He can talk to the elders, can't you?'

Victor nodded – then turned his back and threw up in the bushes.

'Perhaps he's got a bug,' said Bessie, sympathetically.

'Poor bug!' I said.

The youth sprites were approaching fast. A quick decision had to be made – by Bessie!

'AAAAAhhhhrrrggghhh,' she yelled, leading the rest of us into the chorus.

All at once the thick green forest air was filled with the unpleasant mixture of ear splitting screeching and screaming, and intermittent waves of wailing – from Gilbert – stopping Norbert and his gang firmly in their tracks.

Victor emerged from his safety hole. 'fopvhi, qmfbtf! mppl, fmefst dpnjoh opx.' As he spoke the approaching group of younger sprites hastily retreated to the safety of their tree house but watched intently as the elders flew in.

What a sight greeted their curious eyes; a small yet perfectly formed, sprite hating sprite, two fastidiously tidy changelings and four pilp collectors dressed in badly assembled costumes with papier-maché heads – one of whom had to keep a hand on a rip in her suit so her pink knickers didn't show through!

Landing confidently in front of us they circled round, looking us up and down suspiciously, smelling the air that surrounded us. I held my breath as each one came near, hoping they wouldn't suss us out. We'd have to trust Gilbert and Victor to get us through the situation and try to find out the whereabouts of Myrtle. After several minutes they regrouped in front of us then, most surprisingly, they addressed the smallest one by name – and in our language.

'Ah, Victor you come back at last and you got friends too,' said the tallest one with facial warts and a large rounded belly. Behind him, a shorter, greener sprite sniggered loudly and nudged a third one with his elbow. 'Yeah, you bring friends.'

After striking both sprite two and three across the head, the first sprite continued, 'You come with us to see chief. He waiting to see you.'

Victor stepped slowly towards the tall sprite.

Gilbert gasped and stretched out his hand to stop him. 'What are you doing?' he whispered.

Victor heartlessly brushed him aside and joined his kin, shaking the hand of sprite three.

'Yeah, chief said to bring you straight away,' said the sprite as Victor let go of him. 'You gonna get a big reward for this.'

Whoa! Back up a bit, Aggie. Was I hearing this right? I looked around at the others. Their startled eyes, peering out from the make-do sprite costumes, said it all. My head spun as I tried to make sense of what was happening. They were actually waiting for us to arrive? They knew we were coming? It could only mean one thing ...

'Oh my portals, he's a bloody spy!' I whispered

into the ear hole of Gilbert's head piece.

'No, he's just acting so we don't get caught,' whispered Gilbert protectively. 'Just wait and see. He'll put them off. He'll find out where Myrtle is, he will!'

'Why d'you think he was so nervous? All that throwing up ...'

'But he's got a bug, Bessie said so too!'

'Oh Gilbert, look for yourself. See how matey they all are?'

'He's a spy? But why ...' Gilbert's eyes welled up in shock as he realised the truth behind his best friend's actions. 'I don't understand ...'

The rest of our group, apart from the twins, slumped silently to the ground unable to comprehend the moments revelations. Stroppy to the last, I adopted a defiant stance and a fixed glare.

'You two,' said the tall warty one pointing to the changeling sprites, 'take the pilp collectors to the Guest Tower.' At least the twins had got away with it – or had they? We waited anxiously for Victor to correct the sprite but he remained strangely quiet choosing only to stare outwardly to the forest and thus avoid eye contact with us.

'You get what we said, Victor?' said the tall sprite, throwing an arm around the traitor's shoulder as they prepared to take off to see the chief.

'Yes, father – I got it all. I know all the possible

routes to the magic dust and exactly where it's stored.' Victor turned his head slightly, catching the scornful gaze of Gilbert full on.

With anger boiling up inside me I suddenly let rip and launched myself at the 'orphan'.

'You bloody liar! An orphan you said and you speak our language perfectly. After all we did for you – after all Gilbert did for you. I hope you rot, you stinking traitor.' He barely struggled as I clawed at his insipid green skin, with my nails drawing green gunge as the cuts deepened. Even as the shorter sprite yanked me off his back he did nothing. His face, devoid of emotion or remorse, startled me and I too slumped heavily to the ground where the others sat.

I couldn't believe we had been so stupid, so gullible. I tried one more time to reach the Victor we thought we all knew. 'But what about Myrtle? I can't believe you don't really care about her. What have they done with her?'

At last he spoke but these were not words we wanted to hear.

'Myrtle's not here. She was never here. I'm ...' His sentence was left unfinished as the other sprites lifted him up and flew him off to the eastern side of the sprawling forest to collect his reward.

# Chapter Five

Stunned by Victor's parting shot, we sat in a huddle, broken fairies hardly daring to speak. What was there to say? So much time had been wasted and, thanks to Victor, we were still no nearer to finding Myrtle.

Fred tried desperately to console Gilbert but to no avail. His painful sobs cut through the headpiece like a barrier piercer. Victor's betrayal had hit him hardest.

Fred levered the fake sprite headpiece off gently to reveal the shattered remains of his little brother. 'Gilbert, come on mate, calm down. I know this is hard for you, but we've got to get back home.'

Gilbert's reddened eyes barely blinked as he tried to make sense of all that had just happened. 'B-B-But he lied to me, Fred. H-H-He even pretended to be my friend ...'

'He fooled us all – he fooled everyone! But you've got to put it behind you, now. We need to find a way to get back home and find Myrtle. She'll be relying on us to find her. She'll be relying on you!' Fred emphasised Gilbert's role in our mission hoping that his closeness to Myrtle would spur him into action.

Through nodding his head, Gilbert showed some idea of understanding and wiped his watery eyes -

and snotty nose – on the sleeve of his costume.

The twins, not knowing what to do, resorted to what they knew best, tidying up – Gilbert.

'Oh, for goodness sake, you two, leave him be!' said Bessie crossly. 'Can't you see he's upset?'

'We just wanted to make him feel better.' Stan said, trying to smooth down Gilbert's crown tuft, 'Being tidy and clean will help ...'

'I hate to say it,' Fred cut in, 'but these two are probably our only hope of getting out of here.'

The three of us, Fred, Bessie and me, – Gilbert being in no state to do so – stared at the two changelings, deemed to be our saviours, as they wiped the snot and dribble carefully off Gilbert's sleeve, then we looked back at each other.

'Oh, my wingtips! There has to be another way. I mean, look at them – how on earth are they going to be of any use to us,' said Bessie, scornfully. 'Look out sprites, here come the twins and they'll tidy you up if you don't let us go! Oooohh, scary!' She scratched crossly at the ground with a piece of broken twig.

'What choice do we have? We've got to make it work.' I beckoned to the twins, tearing them away from their favourite occupation. 'Right, now listen up you two.' Reluctantly they stood in front of me as I whispered the plan into their large spritey ears. 'You see those sprites in that tree. Those mean looking sprites staring over at us right now?' They nodded. 'Well, if you don't pretend to be sprites taking us to the Guest Tower, they are going to play with us all just like that pilp donor did with you, remember?'

Stan gulped nervously and rubbed his head.

'But we need to finish tidying Gilbert,' said Alf. 'He needs us.'

'Look, when we get back I'll show you the town storeroom. It's a right mess – you'll love it!'

'Okay, what must we do, Aggie?' they said, begrudgingly.

But before I had time to explain, Norbert the nauseous and his hideous henchmen were upon us. In all his revolting greenness, he stood there, hovering over Bessie's back, flicking his fingers on her headpiece. 'xf dpnf up qmbz xjui qjmq dpmmfdupst, zfbi?' He drooled, leaving a long trail of greenish saliva hanging precariously from his mouth.

There was no need for any interpretation – his intentions were perfectly clear!

Aware of the danger, Stan moved in surprisingly fast. 'fs, op! xf up ublf uifn up hvftu upxfs sjhiu opx.' ... and he spoke in spritespiel – a changeling attribute I'd forgotten about! Brilliant, we should be out of here in no time.

Next, Alf stepped forward and pointed at us in

turn. 'Yeah, on you feet, you, er, pilpies. To the Guest Tower.' His imitation of a sprite was almost perfect and his performance was only spoilt by a silly admission of ignorance. 'Mmm, yeah – er,' he said, 'which way is it?'

Oooopps!

'Ey! You not real sprites,' squealed Norbert angrily, sending a trail of sprite slobber into the air as he moved. 'You changelings! Quick, scream alarm ...'

But before he could finish, Fred thrust his hand over the huge mouth preventing any scream from being emitted.

'Here, Fred,' I call-whispered, throwing him a long thin tree root. 'Tie him up.'

Alf and Stan jumped the other one, stuffing his mouth full of fallen leaves and gagging him with strong vines I'd found hanging from a nearby tree. Gilbert took down the third member while I tackled the smallest and final gang member.

'What about their greenness? We need to cover their skin up,' said Bessie.

I looked around but being so dark it was hard to see anything that might be useful.

'How about this?' said Fred, clutching a handful of grey dust from the ground. 'It's not great but it'll do the job.'

'Better than nothing, I suppose,' I said. 'Smother them with it. Make sure no green shows through.'

With each of them gagged, discoloured and firmly bound, we stood back to discuss our next move. The twins, reverting back to *their* normality, began cleaning Norbert's head with his own saliva, mixing the grey dust to a thick paste. Norbert shuddered and flinched with each touch.

'Stop tormenting him,' said Fred, pulling the frightened sprite against a tree.

'You know we're gonna have to take them to the Guest Tower,' I said. 'The sprites will be expecting four creatures of some sort to be brought there pretty soon.'

'But it's too dangerous,' Fred cut in, 'and besides we need to get back to Pilpsville – the sprites are probably going to attack now that Victor's given them inside information.'

'You're forgetting that at the moment we have no way of getting back, remember – no barrier piercer!' Bessie held out her hands in despair. Stan and Alf looked at the ground sheepishly and shuffled their feet in the dirt nervously.

'Look, we weren't having a dig at you two. You've been really brave today.' It was true. We'd seen a different side to the raffle prizes. I continued, 'But you're gonna need to be even braver if we're all to get out of here.'

'We'll do as you say, Aggie,' the twins said in unison.

'You need to find the place where the sprites get into the human world – their crossing – and pass through. Then you'll have to change back into pilp collectors to go through the exit to get back to our world. Then …'

'Or,' said Fred, 'can't we just see if there's a tiny hole where we superglooed the barrier up? If there is, the twins could morph into flies and get through to the other side!'

'Okay, smart ass but let's get these to the tower first. Perhaps we'll get some kind of clue to what's gonna happen.'

'Which way, Norbert?' I said sternly, 'and no lies or we'll set the twins on you.'

Norbert's trembling green finger emerged from his bindings and pointed in the direction of the Guest Tower which apparently, according to Fred, was to the west of the forest.

'Okay, you take Norbert, Fred. Bessie and I will take these two.' I pointed to the two larger members of Norbert's gang.

'We'll manage this one between us, won't we Alf?' said Stan, lifting the front end of the last neatly wrapped sprite.

Fred looked at his brother. 'And Gilbert will help, won't you?'

'But I'm too upset to carry such a heavy weight,' he whinged, wiping yet another tear from his eye.

Fred grabbed the headpiece from the ground. 'Put your helmet on, Gilbert. The twins will have enough to do if we get stopped – unless, of course, you're willing to talk with any sprites that cross our way.'

Thrusting his shoulder midway beneath the heaving load, Gilbert reluctantly agreed then added, 'I never want to speak to another sprite, not ever.'

With the terrified captives firmly tucked under arms and on shoulders we headed off to where the Guest Tower lay. As the ground fell away beneath us we became aware of the immediate landscape. As with any forest, an immense amount of trees was noticeable. But these were different to what we'd encountered before. They towered majestically above the ground like tall, thin poles. Each was topped with a huge plumage of branches which held hand shaped leaves in vast quantities.

'Look at the sparkly lights. That must be where they live,' said Bessie quietly. She pointed up to where tiny green lights twinkled brightly from the tree canopies.

'Yeah, little huts on platforms in the branches,' said Fred as we soared a little higher. 'How sweet!' he added sarcastically. 'That's probably how the humans think we live.'

With darkness still surrounding us, the trees seemed to close in menacingly. In addition, creeping up on us slowly was the green mist which had thickened and risen in line with our flight, clinging steadfastly to our wings like cold porridge. It felt like we were flying through syrup.

'Hell, we'll never make it at this rate,' Fred said crossly, flapping desperately to try and build up speed.

'You're just wasting energy,' I said. 'Calm down – don't flap so much.'

'You know what we need, don't you?' said Gilbert, clearly not suffering from the ill effects of carrying one whole sprite by himself.

'What's – that – then?' panted Fred, struggling terribly to maintain his height under the bulk of Norbert's bound body.

'We need an FFP, like the one Phyllis used,' Gilbert said.

'And – just –-where – will – we – find – one – of – those, – you – twit!' I gasped, angrily.

'Albert's got one,' he said. 'He's got a Fast Flying Pack.'

'But – he's – not – here,' gasped Bessie.

''Who's that then?' said Gilbert, pointing to a tree to the left of us where a very Albert looking face peered out from behind the long, slender trunk. So much for our 'disguises'. He waved then turned, showing his back where the wonderful FFP was strapped. He beckoned us over, gesturing silence with his finger to his lips. The sight of him clearly lifted our spirits and with it came a sudden new lease of flight as we pushed against the thickening mist to reach him.

'Quick, get behind the trunk,' he said, 'I've just seen a patrol of sprites. I think they're looking for them.' On hearing this, the captured sprites wriggled, desperate to get out.

A moss encrusted branch provided a welcome resting place and we hooked up our packages on one of its many notches.

'How did you know it was us?' said Gilbert, stretching out his arms and then his wings.

'You're joking, huh? The state of your outfits I'm surprised you haven't been caught already!' Albert always had a way of making me feel crap! 'Except for those two,' he continued, pointing at the twins, 'they're really well made.'

'Why – are you – here?' I said, getting my breath back at last. 'We were managing fine on our own.'

'Oh, yeah! You really looked like it!' He crossed his arms and laughed. 'You need me Aggie, admit it.'

'No, Albert! We need the FFP!' I said crossly. Why do big brothers always interfere? We were doing just fine – well, I suppose we were struggling a little, just a bit – but never enough to warrant big brotherly intervention! Hmmph!

'How did you get in, Albert?' Bessie asked coyly,

flicking her hair from her eyes as she spoke. She had a soft spot for him and always went weak at the wings when she spoke to him.

'After the nightsgritch I made my way to the barrier border and flew along it then saw some trees neatly labelled with the contents of each trunk.'

We all looked in astonishment at the twins. Even Norbert and his gang lifted their heads in the direction of the changelings.

'You labelled the trees?' I said. 'What if somefairy other than Albert had come along, huh?'

Albert continued, 'Luckily I found the barrier piercer where they'd said so the labelling was useful in that way.'

'And you removed the labels?' I said.

'Of course – I'm not stupid, you know,' he said indignantly.

Hmmm, the answer to that welled up in my throat begging to be released but I swallowed hard knowing this was not the time to pick a fight.

'Okay, so what's the plan?' said Albert.

Blimey, why was it always me who had the plan? I reeled off the simple version of what was likely to happen. 'Well, we've got to somehow get these sprites to the Guest Tower, listen in to find out if they have plans to invade Pilpsville, get back through the impenetrable barrier, seal it up then warn all fairy folk that the sprites are on their way – oh, and the twins are changelings and Victor's a sprite spy! Anything else you need to know?'

Albert's face grew red with fury. His eyebrows twitched in a manner I'd only seen twice before – both times had involved Gertie Cruet.

'Yeah, he's a rotten spy,' splurted Gilbert, 'and he's a big fat liar. I hate him!' he added with venom.

'Calm down, little fairy. We know what he is,' said Fred seeing the sadness once more appear in his brother's eyes. He threw a comforting arm around Gilbert's shoulder.

Albert stared at the ground as if contemplating his next move but then as the anger in his cheeks drained away he spoke again. 'And Myrtle?'

'She's not here,' I said softly. 'She's never been here. It was all a trick to get us to Spercham.'

'Right,' he said, quietly.

I left him alone with his thoughts for a few minutes then had no choice but to interrupt. 'Albert, let me have the FFP so we can get to the tower. If some sprite comes past and doesn't see four tightly bound pilp collectors, they'll start looking for us.'

'I'll come with you. I can haul you all along,' he said.

'But you've no costume. If we're seen …'

'Yeah, you're right. Here!' He pulled the FFP off his back and started strapping it to mine. 'I'll wait here. I need to think anyway.'

'Don't do anything rash. Victor's not worth it. It's Myrtle who's important here,' I said, adjusting the buckles around my waist.

'I just said I need to think. I don't need a lecture!' He tucked himself into the hollow of the tree as we prepared to leave. The long fringe that covered his eyes couldn't mask the anger and frustration that lay within them. He was like a balloon that was waiting to pop. I just had to make sure he 'popped' on the other side of the barrier.

Tucking a sprite back under my arm, I grabbed Bessie's hand, grasping it tightly. She hauled her baggage beneath her remaining arm. 'Fred, you'll have to hold onto my leg. No looking up my dress!'

'As if …' he laughed.

'Oh, whatever!' I pulled the string on the FFP and we were all immediately propelled upwards cutting through the green porridgy mist with ease. After several attempts I managed to assert *some* control over the contraption and we flew in a reasonably straight line towards the tower.

'Come on, Gilbert. Keep up!' Fred call whispered as Gilbert and the twins fell behind a little. With just one sprite between them their load was a lot lighter but the FFP took some keeping up with.

Within minutes the trees ahead of us thinned out and before long we came across an area where just one large tree stood surrounded by the usual thinner ones. It was a strange tree, so different from the others not just because of the thickness of its trunk but by the way its leaves hung down like knives across its branches giving the effect of prison cells. Guarding the solitary doorway, a hole in the middle of the trunk, was a short sprite with an ear infection holding a long, thin stick. He stood grimacing, as he clutched his right ear, on a purpose built ledge that protruded awkwardly from the hole he guarded. Bessie pushed the twins forward with their package. Gilbert hid behind Fred's leg.

'xf'wf cspvhiu tpnf hvftut gps uif upxfs,' said the changelings in unison.

'zpv'wf xibu?' said the sprite, scrunching up its face and pulling what seemed to be a long strip of dirty cotton wool from his ear.

The twins looked to each other then stepped forward until they were just millimetres away from the sprites left ear. 'hvftut!' they shouted.

'bi, zpv cspvhiu nf hvftut up mppl bgufs,' said the sprite.

'Er doh!' said Gilbert, sarcastically from the safety of Fred's leg.

'Sssshh,' whispered Fred, 'You'll give us away,'

But the sprite hadn't heard. In fact it was quite obvious that the sprite hadn't heard anything for a very long time! He was completely deaf!

'tibmm xf csjoh uifn uispvhi?' said the twins.

'zpv csjoh uifn uispvhi,' said the sprite.

'That's what they just said,' remarked Gilbert, interpreting spritespiel without thinking.

The twins gestured to the rest of us to bring forward our burdens. As we passed, the sprite pressed a large green button to the left of the hole. A loud whirring noise preceded the parting of the knife shaped leaves to reveal a small cell resting on the large branch which ran to the left of guard's hole. Along the back of the cell ran a similar line of leaves, closely clinging together in a determined effort to prevent any heroic acts of escapism.

The sprite pointed to the nearest cell, then grabbed Norbert's bound body from Fred with one hand and dragged him to the far corner. He added a badly aimed kick to Norbert's back which slid off catching him in the face.

Gilbert and the twins followed him into the cell, heaving their load through the gap in the leaves.

'kvtu uispx uifn jo' he said to Stan – or was it Alf? 'uifz kvtu tuvqje qjmq dpmmfdupst. xf opu mjlf uifn.'

Gilbert puffed and snorted as the twins translated to the rest of us but remained close to his brother's side. Bessie hauled the bulk of the other gang member through and deposited it roughly next to Norbert. 'Bloody cheek,' she said. 'He's the one throwing his own kind into jail and he calls us stupid!'

Bessie was right. The grey dust had concealed the sprites true identity perfectly and despite what Albert had said about our costumes, the disguises had held – so far. But there was still a problem with Bessie's costume. A bright pink patch stared out for all to see.

'Your knickers are showing again! Cover up that tear before it's seen!' I said, quietly. The sprite might be deaf but there may be others near by so there was no point announcing ourselves.

Bessie blushed slightly before slapping her hand to her bottom to hold the offending tear in place.

'What now?' whispered Fred.

'Give me a hand with this one first,' I said, eager to be relieved of the last remaining sprite bundle.

With Fred's help, I managed to drag the creature across the branch floor where it was left in a heap with the others. It squirmed and wriggled, trying desperately to get free but the bindings were too tight.

The deaf sprite waved us out of the cell then pressed the red button beneath the green one and the knife shaped leaf curtain closed on Norbert and the gang's last performance – at least for a while.

# Chapter Six

After making a quick exit from the Guest Tower using the FFP to gain height and speed through the green mist, we assembled once again behind one of the smaller trees that encircled it.

'I hate sprites!' sighed Gilbert, picking the bark off the trunk and flicking it to the ground.

'Tell me something I don't know,' I said quietly, bored of hearing the same old thing. 'You need to put that hate to some good use instead of taking it out on this poor tree.'

'Aggie's right. Stop moaning while we figure out what to do next,' said Fred, pulling Gilbert gently away from the trunk and settling him on a short stubby branch. He put his finger to his lips to motion silence.

Gilbert crossed his arms sulkily and stared at the ground. 'I was just saying …' he began.

'Well don't,' said Fred, sharply. 'Right Aggie, what are we to do now?'

Deep down I knew we needed to continue our search for Myrtle but it felt as if our business in Spercham was far from over. More importantly, this was an ideal opportunity to find out just what the sprites got up to and what plans they might have for Pilpsville. But before I had a chance to put these thoughts to Fred, Bessie cut in with her own ideas about the situation.

'I think we'd better head back to Albert and go home,' she said, anxiously looking around. 'Something's not right here. I know it's night time but I haven't seen or heard a single thing in these trees since we left the Guest Tower.' She paused then quietly added, 'You'd have thought that Victor bringing home a group of pilp collectors would have been big news wouldn't you?'

Fred nodded his head nervously. 'Yeah, surely there'd be some kind of celebration or something. It's too quiet.'

Looking around for myself I could see what they meant. The silence of the sprite world was eerie, especially as we knew first hand what dreadful noise they really could make when provoked.

'Perhaps they've all just gone to sleep,' said Alf helpfully. 'It must be very tiring being a sprite – all that screeching and fighting.'

'No,' I said, pensively. 'I don't think they're here at all. Bessie, fly up to the top of this tree – see if there's anything there.'

'What on my own?' she said.

'Er, yeah! Unless you want Fred to hold your hand,' I said, knowing that her crush on him had fizzled out some time ago.

'No – I'll take Gilbert instead'. She grabbed Gilbert

from the safety of the stubbly branch and lifted him up as she flew high into the dense canopy of the lofty tree.

'I hope you've got this right,' said Fred. 'We've already lost Myrtle; I don't want to lose those two as well.'

'I'm just trusting my instincts,' I said, then quickly added, 'and we haven't *lost* Myrtle – she's just been misplaced!' I pulled the twins in closer. 'Better stay with me in case I *lose* you too!' The sarcasm in my voice scraped against my teeth as I spoke. Things were bad enough without Fred losing faith in me.

'I'm sorry – I didn't mean it like that,' he said, draping an arm casually around my shoulder. 'I just worry about Gilbert. I know he's a miserable sod but he's still my little brother …'

'Yeah, just like Myrtle's *my* little sister. I know what you mean but you have to trust me,' I said. 'I do get things right sometimes!'

Fred smirked. He knew me far too well. He'd been there, of course, when I hadn't got things quite right too. But his smirk quickly dissolved into a more serious expression as he looked upwards into the dark night sky. The depth of colour spread across the sky like black treacle, making it impossible to pick out the shapes of Bessie and Gilbert.

'What's keeping them?' he said, anxiously.

'It's a long way up, Fred,' I said.

'Well, if they're not down in the next minute ... '

'Look!' I pointed at the two little figures which had come back in to sight. As they flew closer, their fairy features became crisper and it was clear that Gilbert was not happy – saying that, Gilbert was never happy.

He landed with a dramatic flourish, back on the same stubbly branch Bessie had plucked him from some minutes earlier.

'So tell us. What's going on up there?' I said as Bessie landed on the branch next to him.

But before Bessie had time to speak Gilbert butted in. 'It's bad, it's terrible, it's dreadful!' he said, holding the back of his hand to forehead. 'It's the end of Pilpsville as we know it. It's the ...'

'Oh, shut up will you? You always have to go over the top!' said Bessie.

'I was just ...' he said.

'Yes – you were just going over the top,' she wagged her finger in front of his nose. 'Well stop it right now!' Gilbert's mouth sagged in all the right places as his sulk began to emerge. 'And give me the map we found.'

'But you said I could tell them about that.'

'That was before you started going all, all ... over the top.'

Reluctantly, Gilbert dragged a crumpled piece of paperish material from his pocket and handed it over to Bessie. Seeing his saddened face she puffed and tutted then said, 'Oh, come here. Come and say your piece – but no ...'

'... going over the top, I know,' he sighed but he was obviously pleased that Bessie had relented.

'Well, we flew steadily towards the darkness, not knowing what we might find. Danger lurked all around ...'

'Gilbert!' Bessie narrowed her eyes at him.

'Okay, okay!' He sighed again before continuing solemnly. 'There were no sprites up there. We flew onto the platform where they live but no sign of them. They've all gone – somewhere – and judging by the mess, they left in a hurry.'

'A mess did you say? Well, we'd better get up there fast.' The changeling brothers nodded at each other but before their wings had even taken their first beat, I grabbed them both by the shoulder holding them firmly. Removing my hand, I employed a stern look to help keep them in place on the branch next to me. Alf opened his mouth as if to speak but I quickly cut in before he could finish. 'Sshh! Let Fred talk.'

The furrowed brow on the older Trickle brother deepened as he spoke, '... and the map,' Fred asked. 'What's it of?'

Gilbert squealed with morbid delight. 'It's of Pilpsville ...'

'What? Why should they need a map of Pilpsville?

They know where it is,' said Fred.

'If you'd let me finish!' moaned Gilbert.

Fred growled quietly under his breath as Gilbert continued.

'But it's been scribbled on. All the routes and exits to the pilp plant have been drawn on it.' He drew a deep breath as went into the finale. 'And on the back there's a map of Grublin City.'

'We need to get back and warn them,' Bessie said, then added quickly, 'not the Grublins though, let's not warn them.'

'Warn them of what? – That the sprites have been caught in possession of a map?' I took a quick breath then resumed the conversation. 'No, we need to go and find where the sprites are meeting. We've got to see when they plan to attack.'

Five pairs of bemused eyes glared at me.

'What?' I said.

'You've gone all – *assertive* again,' said Bessie.

'Are you saying I'm bossy?'

'Oh, forget it!' She sighed then raised her eyes to the sky. 'So are we going home or have we got to go on a sprite hunt first!'

'Sprite hunt first,' I said apologetically.

'And a little tidy up before we go?' mumbled Stan, rubbing his hands together excitedly.

'Oh, will you give over with the tidying up lark! No tidying up, right!' I said firmly.

Bessie caught my eye and tutted.

'I know, I know! I'm being assertive again.'

Gilbert rocked back and forth on his branch. 'I'm really bored now. Can we go?'

'He's right. Let's get going. It'll be daylight soon,' said Fred, looking up at the already thinning blue sky.

'What about Albert? He'll be wondering where we are,' said Bessie with just a hint of adoration in her voice. What she saw in my brother I'd never know.

'We can pick him up on the way back,' said Fred, abruptly. 'But we've got to find where the sprites are and what they're up to before they return to their platforms.'

Hmmm! Now who was being assertive!

He flapped his wings together impatiently as he prepared to take off. 'We just need to retrace our flightsteps to where we saw Victor go – you coming?'

Gilbert shrugged his shoulders then tucked in behind his brother.

'Hey, wait for us,' called Bessie, grabbing hold of my arm as she took off. The twins followed on behind as we propelled ourselves towards the unknown.

As we flew back to where our adventure in Spercham began, the night sky became increasingly paler, making the vastness of the forest even more apparent. The thick green mist was thinning too, allowing us to conserve the energy of the FFP for later use. Being caught now was a greater possibility and the need to keep out of sight was growing with every wing flap. With dusk lurking dangerously behind each canopy leaf we passed through the trees keeping close to the slender tree trunks.

'Albert should be just across there,' I said as we came to the place where we'd last seen him. 'Hide behind this tree while I go and get him.' Leaving the others behind I carefully flew over to the tree trunk, looking for the hollow where Albert should have been. There was no sign of him. Anxiously, I flew back.

'What's up? Where's Albert?' questioned Bessie.

I glanced around before answering. 'That must be the wrong tree. He's not there. I'd better have another look round.'

I made a move to go but Fred pulled me back quickly. 'No, Aggie, that's definitely where we left him.'

I perched on one of the branches, stunned at the latest obstacle blocking our return to Pilpsville.

'Oh, great – another Lichen lost. I knew this mission was doomed. It'll be you next, Aggie.' Gilbert's cutting remarks were all that was needed to break down my strong exterior and reveal the way I was really feeling. I yanked off my helmet and cried softly into my hands.

'Hey, it's not your fault. Knowing Albert, he's

probably gone off to investigate or something like that,' said Bessie.

'It's just that sometimes I get so tired trying to hold it all together. Good old Aggie. She'll look out for us. Well, who's looking out for me?' I snivelled, wiping my tears with the cleanly pressed hanky passed to me by Alf.

Fred threw his arm around me. 'Don't be daft. We're always here for you – *I'm* always here for you.' He gave me a gentle squeeze which confirmed just how strong our friendship was.

'Come on, put the helmet back on. Let's keep to the plan and find out where all the sprites are. Hopefully we'll come across Albert on the way.' He took my hand and pulled me up to fly beside him, following the same route Victor took some hours earlier.

'I suppose *you'll* have to fly with me,' said Bessie crossly as she grabbed Gilbert's arm. 'And no more nasty comments to Aggie, right!'

'I was only saying what you were all thinking,' moaned Gilbert.

Bessie didn't reply but I could hear her mutter something about 'my poor Albert' under her breath.

I sighed heavily as I thought once more about my two lost siblings. I hadn't realised how much I would miss Myrtle. Okay, there'd been a lot of teasing involved and the name 'Bugface' had been used on many occasions but that was just normal family banter, wasn't it? I sighed again causing Fred to look across at me.

'We will find them,' he said with concern.

'I know but I just wonder what shape Myrtle will be in after all this time.'

We flew on in silence, keeping to the waning shadows as best we could, listening out for any tell-tale clues that would point the way either to Albert or the sprite gathering.

'What was that?' whispered Bessie, pulling up suddenly bedside us. 'I'm sure I heard a scream – Look! There's something over there, between the two tall trees.'

Having fully recovered from my temporary emotional breakdown, the sarcasm flowed freely once more. 'So which two trees would that be, huh? Those two brown ones there or these two brown ones here ...'

'Oh, very funny – just look, through the gap,' she pointed just to the west of where we were and sure enough, lights could just be seen, faintly flickering in the dawn light. And just a few seconds later her scream theory was also proven as a loud screech penetrated our eardrums. We moved in closer.

'It sounds like some kind of contest,' said Bessie as we listened to the clapping that seemed to take place after each horrendous yell.

'And I bet Albert's the prize,' said Gilbert. 'Sprites are like that – and they're liars and cheats and ...'

'Ssshh, you talk too much,' said Fred, obviously embarrassed by his brother's latest outburst. 'Let's just get in as close as possible to see what they're up to.' He pulled Gilbert up by the scruff of his costume, shaking his head and tutting quietly under his breath.

The lights grew brighter as we approached and the screams got louder. Bessie pointed to the canopy of a tree which stood just before where the sprites were. She ushered the twins in front, pressing her finger to her lips as they passed by her. I joined her as we silently moved upwards to our watching post. Fred dragged Gilbert along by the scruff gesturing the need for silence to him.

The chosen tree was ideal in that it provided both a shelter to rest and perfect camouflage. But it in no way prepared us for the shock we were about to receive as we peeped through its many leaves. Just below us was a large clearing shaped in a perfect circle. Around the edges on chairs made from twigs and branches sat row upon row of sprites. On larger chairs sat two huge sprites with circlets of leaves on their heads.

'What's happening? I can't see,' whispered Bessie from behind me. She pushed and jostled for a better position.

'Ssshh, be quiet. They'll hear you,' I whispered back.

I peered around for any sign of Albert but there seemed to be nothing but sprites. There was definitely some kind of screeching contest going on. We covered our eyes with our hands each time a new pair of contestants took their places in the circle's centre.

'Crikey, how much longer?' asked Fred as the fifth pair took their places. The terrible screaming was playing havoc with our more sensitive ears. Then at last it was over and after much clapping and whistling a branch, festooned with ribbons, was handed over to the winner.

We listened in complete silence as the chief addressed the crowd – in spritespiel!

'What's he saying?' I said to Alf.

'He's praising Victor. He's telling them how Victor suffered at our hands so that all sprites could benefit from what he found out.'

'Suffered, my wings,' mumbled Gilbert. 'I'll show him suffering … ' Thankfully Fred already had him restrained so he wasn't going anywhere. 'Enough, Gilbert. You'll just make things worse.'

Then an elderly sprite stepped into the middle and spoke very loudly, gesturing for quiet.

'He's making an announcement,' said Stan.

'Some special guests have arrived,' added Alf.

'Bloody hell! They know we're here,' said Bessie. 'Might as well give ourselves up right now.'

'No, it's not us.' Stan shot a worried look at Alf.

'Who is it? Come on, tell us!' growled Bessie impatiently.

'It's Grublins,' sighed Gilbert. 'Their special guests are Grublins.'

And sure enough, into the middle of the circle stepped a familiar enemy. Even at the height we were, it was hard to mistake their revolting form or disguise their disgusting odour.

'Grublins!' I muttered. 'Bloody Grublins! I might have known.'

'Did you say Grublins, did you?' Bessie's voice trembled as she pushed forward anxiously, shoving Gilbert and the twins to one side.

'Stay calm, Bess,' I whispered. 'Take deep breaths and ... er, look behind you – look at the lovely sunrise.' I tried to hold her back but fear seemed to increase her strength.

She stopped suddenly at the edge of the branch, clinging tightly to a twig stump. Pulling back the leaves that obscured her view, she fixed her gaze on the sight below. All at once her breathing began to slow down and the beads of sweat that had formed on her forehead started to dry up.

'Phew!' I whispered over her shoulder, 'I thought you'd gone and blown it ...'

Unfortunately she had – big time.

'Aarrrggghh Grublins!' she shouted and promptly fainted, falling through the leafy canopy at 100 miles an hour.

'Flapstop, Bess, Flapstop!' shouted Fred.

'No time – quick – dive.' With that, Fred and I closed our wings and jumped.

'FFP, use the FFP,' he mouthed.

I'd completely forgotten about the contraption but quickly pulled on one of its many strings and felt myself propelled downwards, right under the falling body of best friend Bessie. She was safe. But above me, Fred was having major difficulties and flapstopping at a ridiculous speed. I couldn't possibly catch him while holding Bessie in mid air.

'Flap Fred. Flap harder!' I cried, as he whizzed past me.

'Fred!' screamed Gilbert, watching in horror as his older brother plummeted to certain doom. 'I'll save you!'

'No, Gilbert!' I shouted but it was too late.

Gilbert leapt bravely from the safety of the tree, hurling himself towards his brother's speeding body.

Below us, the sprites revelled in the morbid delights of the pilp collector's circus and their death defying tricks. They roared and cheered as we screamed and fell. A truer enemy would have been hard to find.

A sudden terrifying cry came up from a nearby tree. 'Noooooo.' It was Albert! His clothes were torn. His body bruised and bloodied. Sweat had bonded his hair to his face.

'Let me go!' he screamed, his voice echoing around the arena. 'I can save them.' Albert struggled as the two sprite guards held him back from the platform edge.

From the circle below the bemused sprite chief signalled and Albert was released from his captors grasp.

He frantically stuffed some weighty objects from the platform down his trousers, strapped something to his hand and dived off dramatically. The weight pulled him quickly to the ground and with just metres to spare he stopped just in time beneath Fred's lifeless body.

With Fred still in his arms, Albert threw himself across to the other side of the circle but he was too late. Gilbert dropped heavily to the ground. His inexperience at flapstopping had made him misjudge the jump and he fell badly on the outer edge of the circle. He lay in a crumpled heap, blood pouring from the ear of his costume.

I landed swiftly but carefully, leaving Bessie, who was starting to come to, with Albert and ran over to where Gilbert lay. Lifting the headpiece off gently, I cradled his head in my hands and looked around the sprite circle at their sneering green faces. Only one avoided eye contact – Victor!

A river of tears flooded my face as I screamed at him, 'You could have saved him – he was your friend.'

Victor looked around the circle at the sprite faces eagerly awaiting his answer before replying. 'Why would I want to save him? He's a pilp collector. We're enemies.'

His father translated and a loud roar of approval went up from the crowd but when I looked back at Victor, his head was bowed down low, his face moistened with regret. He had really cared for Gilbert after all.

I sobbed as I scooped up the broken body in my arms and carried him back towards where his brother still lay unconscious.

Bessie had come round by now and had watched and listened in horror at the sprites macabre display of pleasure at our downfall.

As I lay Gilbert at her feet she wept bitterly into her hands. 'This is all my fault. Me and my stupid Grublin phobia.'

'No, Bess. I should have come alone as I'd planned. It's down to me.' I shook my head sadly, wishing things had been very different.

'What's down to you?' Fred was awake, his voice slow and slurring. He rubbed his head vigorously, 'Ouch, something caught the back of the neck. Cut right through my headpiece too ...' He looked around, catching the sniggering green faces before reading mine. 'What's going on?' Then came the inevitable question. '... and where's Gilbert?'

# Chapter Seven

'Well?' Fred looked into the faces of the others before coming back to me. 'Where is he?'

As Albert helped to prop him up, I moved Gilbert's limp body gently round to the side of him. He stared in disbelief. 'Is he ...'

Albert nodded then hung his head dejectedly, 'I'm so sorry. I tried to save you both. I just couldn't reach him.'

Fred stroked his brother's hair affectionately, 'You should have saved him, Albert, not me. You should have saved him.'

A strange quietness descended on the arena as Fred whispered to Gilbert and carefully wiped away the blood that had trickled down his face.

The sprites clung to their benches, eyes fixed and mouths hung open. If one tried to talk it was elbowed heavily until it got the message. The Grublins, strangers to this part of the world and its barbaric customs, just stood and stared.

Fred began to gently remove the pathetic excuse for a sprite costume from his brother's body, talking quietly as he moved each damaged limb. As the last evidence of Gilbert the sprite disappeared, Fred looked upon the ravaged body of Gilbert Trickle, pilp collector for the first time. All at once grief consumed him and he let out a pitiful wail.

Uproar returned once more to the arena as sprites yelled and screamed as the latest events unfolded before them. Shaking hands and smirking, they exchanged small objects with each other. It looked as if they had been betting on how long it would take poor Fred to break down in anguish.

Through my tears I scanned along the rows of our tormentors. There was an empty seat where Victor the traitor had been sitting. Had it all been too much for him?

Suddenly a loud ear splitting scream filled the air and on a platform high above, two identical looking sprites shouted down to the assembled throng. In all that had gone on, I'd completely forgotten about the twins.

'Err, stop!' they shouted in their best sprite accents. At once the terrible mocking stopped and the horrendous noise died down. 'We being attacked by, er, piskies ... er, Mr Chief. Huge purple piskies coming through forest at south gate.' The twins waited nervously for a response and it wasn't long coming.

'Oh drat! Always something stop the fun.' He beckoned to a small group of sprites. 'Hp, tpsu ju pvu!' At his command, several of the seated army rose and flew off to the south.

On the platform above, the twins moved around anxiously whispering into each others ears. After a few seconds they tried again.

'Er, the biggest piskie he said ... ' The twins pushed and shoved each other then one shouted, 'He said our chief was the ugliest creature he ever did see!'

With that the sprite chief threw his arms into the air, translating details of the insult directly to his troops.

Immediately they all stood up, stretched their wings and prepared to take off.

'Butt whatt aboutt ourr deall? Mrr Grangerr nott gonna bee happyy iff wee don'tt takee backk aa pilpp collectorr,' screamed the Grublins as the chief lifted up into the air.

'Take your pick. Take them all. We settle up later.' As he took off, he signalled to his crowned counterpart who took the lead and led the sprites to the south of the forest. Looking back he shouted, 'Do what you like with them. We had our fun.'

Looking around at our sorry state, fun was most definitely not a word that could be used to describe the tragic situation we'd found ourselves in.

The Grublins, however, needing no further invitation, turned to face us, rubbing their filthy, stinking hands together.

'Soo whichh onee iss itt too bee, Flibbertt?' said the short one.

The taller one stroked his middle nostril, 'Welll,

hee saidd goo andd fetchh *himm*, didn'tt hee, Globb?'

'Butt wee knowss hee reallyy wantss thatt onee.' He pointed his grubby finger at me. 'She'ss thee onee causingg alll thee troublee.'

Globb grabbed my arm roughly. I was in no position emotionally or physically to fight back nor, indeed, were the others.

'Where will you take me?' I said, weakly.

Flibbertt scratched his head, then frowned. 'Too Grublinn Cityy off coursee. Thenn Mrr Grangerr ...'

The possibility of gaining some news to Myrtle's whereabouts – the real reason why we were here, suddenly brought me back to life. 'So he's escaped then?'

'II neverr saidd nothingg, didd II, Flibbertt? She'ss tryingg too trickk mee. II toldd youu shee wass troublee.'

*CRASH!* The unexpected and clumsy landing of two small identical Grublins brought the short conversation to a halt. They picked each other up and after a quick dusting of their wings they spoke to the other Grublins.

'Err, youu are nott taking herr anywhere. Inn factt youu are relieved off your duties forr, err, giving state secretss awayy.'

'butt II neverr saidd nothingg, didd II Flibbertt?'

'Mr Grangerr has putt us inn charge noww. You mustt return to Grublinn Cityy, er, orr else!'

'orr elsee – doesn'tt soundd goodd, Globb. Bestt wee goo – noww.' Flibbertt made a move to leave but Globb quickly pulled him back.

'Butt how'dd hee knoww soo fastt, huhh, Flibbertt?' he eyed the little Grublins suspiciously.

Flibbertt picking up on Globb's suspicions quickly added, 'Hmm, andd youu don'tt soundd muchh likee reall Grublinss eitherr!' With that, they both stepped closer to the impostors. The two little Grublins looked at each other, coughed nervously then blushed furiously. They began walking backwards as the real Grublins moved in on them.

'Soo youu aree liarrs, huhh!' Globb took a swipe at the twins catching one on the cheek.

From behind the trunk of a tree, a small familiar green voice stepped in just in time – Victor! 'No, they're not liars. I sent a mind message using a telepathica. My father keeps the creature for emergencies. You must return through the sprite portal to Grublin City as soon as possible.'

'Butt theyy don'tt soundd rightt,' complained Globb, disappointedly.

'We've hadd a dose off Grublintituss,' the twins said, coughing and spluttering for added effect.

The Grublins pondered a while then agreed to return home. 'II toldd youu wee shouldd goo, didn'tt II?' said Flibbertt as they headed off. 'Noww wee gonnaa bee inn bigg troublee.'

With both the sprites and the Grublins gone, we were all alone – at last! Just Victor stood between us and home but with a last glance at the body of Gilbert, he too disappeared.

Albert was the first to speak and break through the depressing atmosphere. He moved over to where the twins stood, patting each one on the back as he spoke. 'Well done, Alf – you too, Stan. I'm sorry we treated you so badly when you first arrived. You've been a huge help but just one more thing. Can you go and unseal the barrier again?'

The twins, now back to their normal selves, nodded in unison. 'Yes, Albert. We'll find the barrier piercer and open the gap.'

Besides Albert knelt Fred, still leaning over Gilbert and straightening out his clothes.

'Come and have a drink, Fred,' I said, offering a flask of cold smint tea from Albert's backpack. The oldest Trickle brother dragged himself up from his brother's side and made his way over to me, grasping the flask gratefully. His sad eyes were dull and bore no reflection as he sunk down against a tree trunk.

I looked over at Bessie who was standing over by the sprite thrones. 'So nice of Victor to pop up and help!' I said sarcastically. 'A little sooner would have been better, huh Bess.' But Bessie was far away in thought, staring at the lifeless body lying in the centre of the arena.

'Come on, Bess. We'll get him back to his mum ...'

She cocked her head to one side. 'Did you see that?'

'Yes, Bess, I saw it all. That Victor had some nerve.'

'No, did you see him wink?' She was still staring at Gilbert.

I took a closer look. 'No, he's still dead.'

'I'd swear he just winked.'

'No, Bessie – he can't wink.' I took her arm gently. 'It's just an involuntary muscle movement. He's gone through the final portal in the sky, up to the greatest healer of all.' I ushered her a little closer hoping that the reality of Gilbert's death would sink in. 'Look for yourself, Bess.' We stepped gingerly in front of his deathly white body. 'There, see – just as I said, he's deceased ...'

'So why's his flipping eyebrow twitching?' Bessie bent over Gilbert's face.

'It's a spasm, Bess – let it go ...'

'LOOK!!' she screamed, shoving my face into that of the dead pilp collector.

The corpse slowly opened its eyes. 'I'm not dead,' it whispered.

'Aaaaarrrggghh,' I screeched, falling back over my feet, landing hard on my bottom. 'You little sod! We thought you were dead.'

Bessie swiped the living corpse across the head. 'Look at the state of your brother!'

Fred lifted his head. 'Gilbert! You're alive?' Finding a new stream of energy, he leapt to his feet and ran over to where Gilbert lay. 'But you were dead. I saw all the blood dripping from your ear and your breathing had ...' He leant over and gave his brother a huge hug.

'Oh, yuk! Get off me!' said Gilbert, 'You stink!'

'Well, that drop was enough to make anyfairy break into sweat!' Fred smelt his clothes, 'Anyway, how did you manage to survive such a fall? Are you badly hurt?'

Gilbert, with Fred's help, pulled himself to his elbows then finally sat up. He opened his clenched fist to reveal a circular wooden object with a small protruding wire. Fred looked at it, puzzled then reached out for it.

'Don't touch it, Fred,' said Gilbert. 'I'll tell you all about it later.'

I left them alone and with Bessie, went over to find Albert who had sat himself down on one of the sprite thrones. He looked lost in thought as we approached but lifted his head and smiled broadly as we drew nearer.

'Good news, huh?' he said. 'Typical Gilbert!'

'Yeah, but he's still a bit woozy from the fall,' I said.

'Least he's not dead!'

'Well, yeah – there's that!' I rolled my eyes towards

the sky, then remembered the question I'd been waiting to ask him. 'Albert, how did you manage to get to Fred so quickly?'

He opened his hand to reveal a copy of his latest invention, the anti-flapstopper, just like the one Myrtle had been trying out a few days earlier.

'and you gave one to Gilbert too … '

'Yeah, but I didn't know if it would work. I hadn't fully tested out that model.'

'Well it obviously worked as he's still in one piece – well almost!' I shuffled my feet and swallowed hard. The next sentence wasn't going to be easy for me to say. 'You're a really good inventor, Albert. Your contraption – the anti-flapstopper – saved Gilbert's life, you know.'

'Oh, my portals. Are you actually giving me some credit, Aggie Lichen?' He smirked then winked at Bessie.

'Well … I suppose … perhaps … oh, shut up!' I was that relieved with the outcome of the expedition that I almost hugged him – then common sense kicked me in the leg and the true reality of our relationship slapped me hard round the face.

'Mind you, the way you're dressed you'd have thought somefairy had died anyway.' Albert eyed my clothing up and down, 'and what are those socks all about?' He pointed at my black and white striped socks and pulled a face.

'Oh my wings – could you *be* anymore last century? I'm a goff. G-O-F-F, goff. Got it!'

Bessie made a move to join Fred. She knew better than to get between me and Albert when arguing. But this was only friendly banter – he'd pay later!

'Right c'mon,' said Albert, springing from the throne. 'The twins should be ready for us now. Let's get young Gilbert home.'

Fred, on hearing this got to his feet. 'We'll need something to make a stretcher.'

'Will this do?' shouted Bessie, holding up a large piece of bark she'd just peeled off a tree. She carried it over to where Gilbert was and together we carefully levered him onto the makeshift stretcher.

'Oooh, this isn't terribly comfortable, you know,' moaned the patient.

'Oh, he's off,' I said. 'Didn't take him long to get back to his groany self!' I added, grabbing hold of the back end of the bark with Fred. Then with Albert and Bessie up front, we took off and headed towards the clearing where the gap in the impenetrable barrier lay waiting.

# Chapter Eight

On the other side of the barrier, no welcome awaited us. In fact nofairy had realised we'd gone which I suppose was a good thing. With the gap carefully sealed, I headed for home with Bessie and the twins, leaving Fred and Albert to fly Gilbert up into the canopy of the sacred oak tree where the healers lived. Once they'd worked their magic on Gilbert he'd be as good as new – certainly better and hopefully less miserable!

'I'm shattered,' said Bessie.

'Why don't you go home and rest? You can catch up with us later, can't she ...' I said, turning to look at the twins. But where the twins had been were two revolting creatures. Both had Grublin bodies and sprite heads. Then they changed. This time sprite bodies with pilp collector heads. It was grotesque.

'Oh, my wings. What's happening to them?' cried Bessie, hiding behind me. 'Ah, Grublin!' she added as they changed again.

'Bloody hell! We'd better get them home quick.'

They were inter-morphing – and it wasn't pretty!

********

'Come on, we'd better stick them in the shed to calm down,' said Pa, seeing the state of the two changelings as he opened the front door to us. 'I'd always suspected there was more to them. Being able to morph is a great gift – just don't let Ma see them while they're doing the, er, weird bit. She'll have a fit.'

We did as Pa said, leaving a few cushions behind for the twins to eventually settle down on. Bess hid behind the door clutching at the handle in fear. She was too frightened to look at the twins in their dreadful inter-morphing modes.

'I see she's not with you,' said Pa, sadly. His eyes grazed the ground as we walked back along the path to the house. 'We'll find her soon I expect,' he added trying desperately to sound optimistic but failing miserably.

As we stepped through the kitchen door, Ma rushed over and hugged me and Bessie tightly. 'Oh, I'm so glad to see you two – and where's Myrtle hiding, huh? No, don't tell me – she's gone to have a lie down. Well, that's okay, I'll go and make her a nice hot cup of ...'

'She – she wasn't there, Ma.' I swallowed nervously as I broke away from her.

'What do you mean?' Her face suddenly paled and she fell back onto the kitchen chair in shock. 'But you were going there to find my Myrtle and bring her home,' she said sadly.

'I'm sorry, Ma but the sprites never had her after all.' I threw myself on the chair next to her.

Her eyes, full with tears, fell to the floor. Pa reached over to comfort her. 'Come on, love. I think a lie down will do you good.' He pulled Ma up and guided her towards the door. 'I'll not be long. Then you can talk to me about your adventures in Spercham – and what we ought to try next.'

Bessie sat down next to me, elbows on the table and cupping her face in her hands. 'What *are* we going to try next, Aggie? Any ideas?'

'Don't know, Bess.' I leant heavily on the table, crossing my arms and resting my head on them. 'Right now,' I yawned, 'I just feel so tired. I just want to sleep ...'

********

'What time is it?' I asked sleepily, waking up from my nap. 'And how did I get here?' I pulled the pillow up behind my head as I sat up in bed.

Ma pushed a hot cup of gurge soup into my hands. 'Albert brought you in.' She stroked my hair as she spoke.

A pang of guilt rose in me. 'Ma, I'm sorry I didn't find Myrtle. We did look, honest. We ...'

'It's okay, Aggie. I shouldn't have built my hopes up like that. And of course you looked – Albert's filled us in with all the dreadful details including all about that little sod Victor!'

'Oh no!' I said, thrusting the cup back at Ma. I threw the bedclothes off desperately.

'Whatever's wrong?' cried Ma, wiping specks of hot soup from her hands.

'The-The-The sprites! They're going to invade. They could be on their way right now!'

'Hey, you sit back down!' She placed the cup firmly back in my hand. 'It's all been taken care of. We got word to Mr Fettock. He's organising patrols all over Pilpsville.'

'But Victor knows everything about the pilp plant.'

'It's all covered.' She sighed heavily. 'We could have lost you too, then what would we have done?'

I slurped noisily on the hot soup trying not to think about what could have happened. A change of conversation was urgently needed. 'Is Bessie still here?' I said.

'No,' said Pa, popping his head round the door. 'Her mum came for her some time ago. She said she'll be back after she's rested.' He came in and sat on the bed. 'And how about you, Aggie Lichen, how are you holding up?'

'Oh, I'm fine now that I've had a sleep,' I said, finishing off the last dregs of soups.

'It's okay to cry, you know.' He leant forward and patted my hand. 'We know what you've been through.'

'No, it's fine, honestly.' Besides, there was no way I'd cry with Albert looking in through the door crack!

'Right then,' said Ma, 'as you're feeling okay, let's get you up and out of these dreadful dark and dingy clothes – did somefairy die, dear?'

I rolled my eyes to the ceiling and bit down hard on my tongue. 'I can manage myself, Ma,' I insisted, trying to prise her eyes away from my dark attire.

'She's right, Ma. Let's leave her to get sorted. There's a nice cup of smint brewing in the kitchen.' Pa smiled at her and realising I needed some waking up space, they headed off to the kitchen.

For the next ten minutes or so, I sat transfixed at the mirror on the dressing table in the room I used to share with Myrtle. It seemed so long since I'd last seen her or heard her voice. I missed her. I missed her irritating snoring and the annoying way she flapstopped constantly. I missed our arguments – I missed calling her Bugface. I sighed deeply as I thought about it and would have sunk into an even deeper depression if a loud knock on the bedroom door hadn't quickly brought me back to reality.

'Yeah,' I shouted, frantically wiping the tears from my eyes. 'What is it?' I grabbed some of the pale face powder I'd recently bought and dabbed it over my eyes. The redness diminished rapidly.

'You'd better come, Aggie,' said Albert, poking his head round the door, 'We've got another note.'

I threw on the rest of my clothes – black of course – grabbed my boots from the bottom of the bed and rushed out the bedroom, down the hallway.

As the kitchen door swung open I was greeted with a now familiar sight. Ma sobbing heavily, Pa comforting Ma as best he could while Albert, propped against the wall, read silently through the kidnap note.

'Oh, hell! What does this one say?' I said, standing on tip-toes to read over Albert's shoulder.

'Here, see for yourself,' he said, thrusting the paper in my hand. 'It's not good news.'

I read through the note astonished at the sheer cheek of Myrtle's captor. 'He wants what?'

'5000 credits … and the anti-flapstopper patent!' Albert shook his head in dismay. 'If he gets that, he could make a fortune. That was supposed to be my way of making some decent credits.'

I looked at him, raising my eyebrows.

'For all of us not just me!'

'But now … you'll give it up?' I said, knowing how important this particular invention was to him.

He squeezed the back of the kitchen chair hard. The white in his clenched knuckles displayed his anger at the kidnapper's demands. 'What choice do I have, huh?' He shrugged his shoulders, shoved his hands deep into his pockets then headed out the door and off to his bedroom.

'Hey, hang on. What about this bit at the bottom? It says *I* have to deliver it all in person. Why me?'

Slam!

Albert had heard enough.

'Pa, did you see this? He wants *me* to take everything to him. He'll kill me, you know he will ...'

A head appeared at the door. 'Oh, I think that's going a bit too far!' Ferrett Granger, his beard tangled, his grey hair windswept and standing to attention, strode into the room and took up the chair next to Ma. 'I heard you'd returned so I thought I'd call round to see how it all went.'

'Well, first ...,' I begun.

'The shortened version will do,' said Ferrett, combing his hair back into place and de-tangling his facial hair.

So in as few words as possible I recounted our time in spriteland and consequently, our failure to find Myrtle. Ma, who had settled by now, turned round to face me with Pa.

Ferrett politely sprinkled the conversation with some 'mms' and 'ahs' as he listened. 'So you're not actually any closer to finding Myrtle than before?'

'Well, if you put it that way – no!' I picked at a loose fingernail I'd broken on some Spercham Forest bark.

'And the new note ... what's that got to say?' he asked, taking the note from my hand. 'Ah, credits and a contraption too! And you're to take them to the kidnapper.'

'To Arty,' I cut in. 'I'm to take them to Arty – alone.'

'But he's still at Mursham Marshes – remember, I told you that last time ...' he said.

'But in Spercham,' I argued, 'the Grublins said they were working for Arty. That's why they were there.'

'Well something's amiss here,' he said, examining the note closely.

'What do you mean?' said Ma becoming agitated once again.

'Well, for one thing – I can't say I recognise this writing as Arty's.' Ferrett held the note up to the light. 'And why would he want the patent to an anti-flapstopper? As for the credits demand, first it was just 100 credits and now its 5000.' He scratched his beard before continuing. 'It's as if the creature responsible is building a shopping list! It just doesn't sound like Arty.'

'No, it's him alright. I'd bet my last pilp on it. I remember that look he gave me as he was taken away to prison. And ...' I added, 'he asked for me to take the ransom to him – me.'

'It doesn't say where or when to meet though,' said Pa.

'Look carefully at the bottom, Pa,' I said.

Pa held the paper nearer to his eyes and read the

untidy scrawl at the bottom. It looked as if it had been added as an after thought. 'It says to put everything in a backpack and keep it with you at all times. You will be contacted with the exact meeting point.'

'So I'm supposed to fly round with 5000 credits on me, huh?' I said crossly.

'Don't be silly. Where would you get 5000 credits from? No offence meant.' Ferrett smiled sweetly at Ma and Pa.

'No, you're right, Ferrett. Surely Arty would know that,' said Ma.

'I suggest you just put the other things in your backpack – and I'll write a note to cover the 5000 credits.' Ferrett reached in his pocket for a pencil.

'But you said not to pay …' I began.

'Oh, I'll not honour it, no, no, no! It's just a bluff!' He scribbled away on a piece of paper then handed it over to me. 'Whoever's behind this will get a nasty shock if they try to cash it in!'

'You mean, Arty. *He'll* get a nasty shock,' I said.

'Perhaps you're right.' He pushed his pencil firmly back into his pocket then stroked his beard thoughtfully. 'Might I suggest a little detour in your quest to find Myrtle.'

'We haven't really got the time,' I said quickly. 'We need to plan our next move.'

'Ah, but before we do anything hasty it may be a

good idea go to Pershador.' He tapped his finger on the ransom note several times. 'You should consult one of their readers. They should be able to determine who the kidnapper is easily.'

'So why didn't you suggest that earlier? We've wasted all that time going to Spercham Forest. Gilbert nearly died ...' I said angrily.

'We were all so sure that Myrtle would be with the sprites, weren't we? Besides, you found out that Victor wasn't exactly who he said he was.' Ferrett stared straight into my eyes. 'Surely that was useful?'

'You knew all along, didn't you?' I said.

'I had my suspicions but none of you would believe me if I'd said anything – You were all too close.' He smiled, 'Even you!'

He was right. There'd probably been a stream of tell-tale signs that we'd all ignored because we'd trusted Victor. He'd been one of us.

'So to Pershador then!' said Ma, breaking my thoughts. 'You'll need to leave straight away.'

'What about school?'

'Oh, of course – you wouldn't know. It's closed 'til further notice. Somefairy has blocked all the toilets with pilp imitators. We've already had a power cut because they'd got into the pilp plant system.'

'Grublins! It'll be Grublins – it's always Grublins.' Bessie stumbled in through the back door bringing the twins, who had 'escaped' from the shed and seemed back to normal, with her. 'Smelly, horrible things those Grublins. They're everywhere. Probably near by r-right n-now ...'

'Oh, she's off! Aggie, get a brown bag – quick.' Ma stood in front of Bessie and started breathing exercises.

From the cupboard drawer I grabbed a bag and passed it to Bessie who then went through her well practiced routine of deep breathing.

Ma carried on her earlier conversation. 'So you're okay to go straight away? Are you listening to me?'

'I'm sorry, Ma. The twins were twitching. 'I think they're gonna morph again. I can't concentrate.'

Stan and Alf held their breath to try and control themselves but with their other characters so desperate to get out, it was an impossible task. And every time they morphed into a Grublin Bessie screamed.

'Albert put them in the new bedroom – and cover the mirror or they'll scare themselves half to death!' said Pa.

'New bedroom, huh! So there are some advantages in winning the raffle then?' said Ferrett.

'Have them both,' said Ma. 'The twins and the bedroom!'

Ferrett laughed and nodded his head vigorously causing his long beard to swish to and fro. 'No, you're alright. I think keeping tabs on my nephew is enough for me to cope with.'

Ma threw him a look which could have been translated as – perhaps if you kept a greater eye on Arty, things would not have got into this state.

Bessie lifted her head out of the brown bag at last.

'So where are we going now?' she asked, lowering her bag.

'Pershador,' I announced.

'Pershador! They have all sorts of weird people there, like mind readers and ...'

'Yes, Bessie – Pershador. Ferrett thinks it would be good to talk to the readers there about the notes that have been arriving. Don't you Ferrett?' said Ma.

Ferrett at last able to break away from Ma's glare, nodded and looked at Bessie as he spoke. 'They should be able to pinpoint where it was written and possibly who by.'

'They'll pinpoint a lot more than that if they get inside our heads – they'll suck your brain out if you're not careful too!' Bessie shuddered, 'Yuk!'

'Suck your brain out indeed,' laughed Fred, peering in through the window. 'They'd have to find it first!'

Bessie rushed over to the open window and thrust her face into his. 'Mmmm, very funny Mr Trickle. You just wait ...'

'Well I think that's the point, actually,' I said, grabbing the backpack Ma had been preparing. 'We can't wait. Come on, we need to go now!'

'What about Albert? Is he coming?' Bessie asked, twiddling her hair round her fingers – a sure sign that she was still sweet on him.

'No, just us three. He's doing the nightsgritch.' I looked at Fred who had just come in through the back door. 'I'm assuming that's why you're here – to go with us?'

Fred nodded, took the backpack from me and threw it over his shoulder.

'Don't forget this one!' Albert thrust another backpack at us. It was much bulkier and heavier than the other one. 'It's got the FFP in it ... and the anti-flapstopper patent!' He scowled as he spoke revealing the full extent of his feelings about parting with his precious belongings.

'Don't forget this,' said Ferrett passing the 5000 credit note to me with a smirk. I stuffed it in one of the bags pockets.

'You'd better take the twins too,' said Pa. 'They could come in useful – when they stop morphing!'

The twins appeared at the kitchen door with Ma. 'I've given them both a dose of Ketrin. It may help to slow the morphing down but until then just try and keep them out of sight. Fairy folk are not used to seeing changelings around here.'

'Ahh, Grublins!' shrieked Bessie, as the twins morphed again.

'Best keep them away from her too!' added Ma.

As we made our way to the front door, Pa pulled me to one side. He waited until the others were out of sight then handed me a small package. 'I forgot I had this still,' he whispered, tapping the side of his nose with his forefinger. 'Only if you *really, really* need it though.'

I gingerly unwrapped the grubby muslin cloth, peeling back the corners to reveal – a tatty wooden whistle! I looked at him, puzzled.

'Storm Troopers!' he said, his voice low yet full of intrigue. 'They will come if you call – but be sure that it's absolutely essential, for with every blow comes a consequence.'

I wanted to laugh out loud but he was deadly serious. Storm Troopers indeed! They were the stuff of folk tales yet here was my Pa insisting that I take the 'magic' whistle just in case. I tapped the side of my nose echoing his earlier gesture of secrecy. 'Okay, Pa. I'll keep it in my pocket.' I slipped it quickly in the dark depths of my jacket, patting it gently into position.

'Be careful – make sure it doesn't fall into the wrong hands – dire consequences!' He tapped his nose again then escorted me to the front door to where the others were waiting.

We said our goodbyes and made off through the back door flying high amongst the trees to cover our movements. Fred and Bessie flew in front so that she couldn't see the twins who flew with me. Unfortunately she always seemed to turn her head at the wrong moment. Consequently, the journey was littered every few minutes with shrieks of 'Ahhh, Grublins.'

'How long before we reach the border?' called Fred, after we'd been airborne for about an hour, 'Only I could do with a break from her screaming in my ear every two minutes!' he pointed at Bessie in disgust.

'I can't help it!' she said, 'It's just that every time they morph into ... aahh, Grublins!'

'See what I mean?' he said.

'It should only take about another hour,' I said, looking around at the twins who were just in the process of morphing into sprites for the eighth time. 'They're definitely slowing down. I've only seen the sprite morph twice in the last 20 minutes,' I added, desperate to continue our journey.

'I really think we need to stop. The twins look exhausted,' Fred insisted.

Reluctantly, I agreed. 'Alright, but just for a few minutes.'

We took refuge in a nearby shret tree, placing Bessie on a branch well away from Stan and Alf. I gratefully pulled the bulky bag off my back and shuffled along the branch next to Fred. 'Right, let's see what Ma's packed in that bag, Fred.'

He unzipped the bag and poked about. 'Usual stuff – drinks, cakes ...' He threw the twins and Bessie a cake each then opened a pack of sandwiches for us to share.

We sat for a while making quiet conversation while downing the feast Ma had provided. But as the time went on I felt increasingly uncomfortable – as if we were being watched. Perhaps Arty was ready to collect his ransom.

'Ssshhh! What's that noise?' I said, moving further up the branch to look around.

Bessie flew over. 'What's up?'

'Something's out there. Just behind that rock.' I pointed to a moss covered rock that sat some 100 metres or so from where we were.

'What if it's Arty?' said Bessie reflecting my own thoughts.

'No, this has been following us since we left Pilpsville,' said Fred, 'I smelt it long ago.'

'Smelt it? What the hell is it?' Bessie asked, trying desperately to concentrate on the conversation and not look over at the morphing twins.

'I'm not sure. I haven't really caught sight of it yet,' he creased his forehead in thought, 'Hmm – just the smell ... hang on. Is it greeny-yellow and wispy?'

I poked my head round the tree again to have a further look. 'Now you say it – well, yeah.'

'I might have known! – Gilbert, come here now.' Fred stood up, adopting a hands-on-hips pose.

'Gilbert?' I said.

'Yes! Gilbert,' said Fred. 'He's obviously made some kind of bargain with the healers again!'

The greeny-yellowy wisp swirled out from the rock and headed straight for Fred, the revolting aroma knocking him clean off his perch and onto another.

Within seconds the wisp lost its transparency and in its place was the fairy form of Gilbert. Plasters covered various parts of his exposed body and a large bandage had been wrapped tightly around his head.

'Look at the state of you. Are you sure you should be here?' I said remembering the extent of his injuries.

'It looks worse than it is. They said I'll be fine after a few days rest.'

'So shouldn't you be resting?' said Bessie.

'I rest when I'm the smell. It's not as hard as flying.'

'Crikey! That's a new one,' said Fred, who seemed less astonished at his brother's quick recovery than we were. 'So now you can transfer back and forth into a smell, huh?'

'Well, not always. It'll wear off completely after a week,' said Gilbert.

'That's good then.' Fred patted him on the

shoulder in a brotherly fashion.

'Well sort of – you see when it does finally wear off I could be left as Gilbert or the smell. I won't know 'til the week is up.'

'What! That's a bit of a risk, isn't it? What did you go and agree to that for?' said Fred.

'I just wanted to be able to change into things – like the twins.' He pointed to Stan and Alf who were just in the process of morphing into a sprite. He shrugged his shoulders then went and sat next to them, watching each morph intently.

'Well I suppose the good news is that he's alright … and the other good news is that I could end up with a smell for a brother! What will mum say?'

'He could come in useful – like last time,' I said, recalling Gilbert the smell's heroic achievements in rounding up the sprites during the last invasion.

'Perhaps …' Fred picked up the backpack and pulled it over his shoulder once more.

To the others, this signalled that we were on the move again and they gathered around.

'Just one hour, yeah?' he grimaced, pulling Bessie up next to him.

I grinned and nodded, 'Look straight ahead, Bess. Hopefully the twins will be all morphed out pretty soon!'

# Chapter Nine

The hour passed smoothly enough. Okay – it *was* punctuated with Bessie's fearful cry but by the time we reached the border, the changelings had at last stopped morphing.

'There,' said Fred, pointing to the neat white picket fence which surrounded the land of Pershador. 'They've got a gate keeper though. I'm not sure if they'll let us in.'

'You call that a gate keeper! That woman must be all of eighty! How's she a gate keeper?' I sneered.

'Hey – brains – sucked out, yeah?' said Bessie, tapping her head. '... with a straw ...'

But it was a peculiar sight – an old lady sitting in a white wooden sentry box, knitting. Her grey hair piled up in a bun, her glasses perched on the end of her nose and she was dressed in a uniform of blue and gold. As we drew nearer the ageing lines on her face became more prominent and defined like the canyons of a well lived life. Hell, I thought, you could flow a river through those and still have room for a canoe!

'I think that's a tad rude, dear – don't you?' said the gate keeper, putting down her knitting needles and standing – well bending – up. 'These 'canyons' represent the many minds I have read. It is a small price to pay for my gift!'

'Er, sorry. I didn't mean to upset you,' I said.

'Well, if you can't have a kind thought best not to think at all!' said the old lady gate keeper straightening her uniform as she spoke.

'That shouldn't be difficult,' giggled Bessie, nudging Fred in the ribs with her elbow. Fred mimicked her and elbowed her back.

'And you young man,' she said, looking straight at Gilbert who had his hands shoved deep in his pockets and was kicking the ground – as usual. 'How about some happy thoughts? Your whole mind is full of misery. Cheer up for portals sake! You make mind reading quite depressing – now why are you here?'

'You mean you don't know?' I said, sneeringly, looking around at the others.

'Ah, sometimes it's just polite to ask,' she said, chuckling to herself. 'It's Myrtle, yes? You've lost her, huh?'

'Not *lost* – just, kind of, misplaced,' I said guiltily, twisting my fingers together.

'And you've come here to speak to the readers,' she said, sitting down once more and resuming her knitting.

'We just want to see ...' I began.

'... if they know where she might be?' She finished off my sentence perfectly.

'Well, yeah – can *you* tell us?'

'No, no, no – I'm just a gate keeper. I can read minds, to some extent, but finding a lost pilp collector requires much greater power than I possess.' She stood up once more and took out a small black furry book from her skirt pocket. It hissed and spat as she opened it. 'Be still Patch,' she said as the book threw its long tail out from the centre. We gasped as its paws unfolded revealing huge talons sharpened to a point. 'It's rude to stare,' said the gate keeper.

'But that book's alive – I mean that book's a cat!' I said, startled at what I'd just witnessed.

'A small puma, dear. Did you not listen in school? It was brought over from the other side where the humans live. Poor thing, they'd killed it and made it into a notebook.'

'And now it's alive?' I peered over her arm as it's tail swished menacingly.

'It's all part of the magic of Mirvellon – You really didn't pay attention in class, did you dear? I've tried everything to get him back to normal, unfortunately he's still a notebook!'

'Cool!' said Gilbert stepping forward for a closer look. 'Hey, he nearly got me!' he cried as the notebook took a vicious swing at him.

'I never said he was tame now did I?' She flicked back and forth through the book. 'Anyway, getting back to the readers. I'm afraid nofairy's allowed to see the reader without an appointment ... and you don't seem to have one.'

'What's to stop us flying straight over you and into the city?' said Fred. His patience was wearing thin by the sound of it – much like the rest of us.

She smiled sweetly. 'Hmm, well nothing really – except the membrane of course.'

'Which does what?' said Fred, crossing his arms and frowning deeply.

'It keeps all the outside voices out – too much mind reading can blow your brains out. Oh, and electrocutes any prowlers or pilp collectors trying to sneak in without an appointment!'

'Okay! Okay! When's the next appointment?' I shrieked.

After flicking back and forth once more for the best part of five minutes, she finally spoke. 'Hmm, now let me see – Ha ha! I think we've had a cancellation.'

I clenched my teeth together, trying not to think terrible thoughts about her and a giant food mixer! 'And ...'

'She could see you ... 4 o'clock ... '

I breathed a sign of relief and relaxed. 'That's okay, we'll wait.'

'... next Friday.'

'What! That's no good. We need to see the reader

now. My sister's been missing for ages! You've got to let us in!'

Gilbert kicked the picket fence angrily. I just thought of the food mixer. The old woman frowned.

'Well, like I said, I've nothing until ...' She stopped and turned suddenly to talk to another old woman who had just walked up behind her. A long red cloak with a huge red hood covered her face completely.

'But I've told them – there are no appointments!' the gatekeeper protested.

The red hooded woman whispered in the gate keeper's ear, her hood bobbing up and down rapidly.

'Well no-one told me that today was a non-appointment day! I have all these times allocated you know.' She pushed the black cat book into the other woman's face causing her to jump back as the lethal paws struck out. 'It's all there, you know.'

The hooded woman took her by the arm then thrust a piece of paper in her hand pointing to what looked like a signature at the bottom.

'Looks like we're not the only ones receiving strange notes!' I whispered to Fred.

The gatekeeper backed down at last. 'Okay! I'll send them through. It would just be nice to know in advance next time.'

The old woman in the red cloak beckoned us through the gate and into the city.

'Not the changelings!' said the gatekeeper as we

went to pass. 'They mess with the reader's thinking.'

'Stay here, you two. We shouldn't be long,' I said, sitting the twins firmly on the ground by the fence. 'And don't wander off.'

I hurried to join the others who were now tucked in behind the hooded woman.

'Food mixer, indeed!' said the gate keeper as I passed.

'What did she mean by that?' asked Bessie.

'Just a recipe I had in my head,' I said, not feeling bothered to explain in any great detail.

We followed the red hooded woman further inside. There was a small hexagonal shaped courtyard with colourful fountains in the centre which grew taller and taller until they touched the membrane. Then after a spectacular display of blue sparks they dropped dramatically just to start over again. On each of the six sides was a door, all in different colours. We were led towards the red door.

'Red for danger!' said Gilbert gloomily, as we passed through into a large reception area.

'Oh, shutup!' I said as we approached the desk where another old lady was sat filling in some forms. 'You always have to say something bad, don't you? We're going to find out where Myrtle is at last. That's good, right?'

The red hooded woman disappeared through a door to the right of the desk. Pinned to it was a badly spelt hand scrawled poster saying, 'nock befor entring'.

'Just take a seat,' said the receptionist. 'I'll be with you in a couple of tocks.'

'Doesn't she mean ticks?' whispered Bessie.

'No, she means tocks,' said Fred. 'Listen.' And he pointed to a tall red clock from which came loud tocks every second.

'Oh, what's it matter?' I said crossly. 'We've still got to wait around again! We just don't seem to be getting any closer.'

'Look, this could be it. This reader could know exactly where Myrtle is,' said Fred, trying to comfort me. 'Then we can fly straight to her and take her home.'

I sighed then slumped back on one of the red chairs that lined the room and sat next to Gilbert. To pass the time, I resumed our earlier conversation. 'So why can't you just try to be happy – just for once, huh?'

'It's this place. It's too ...'

I cut in before he had time to finish. ' ... colourful? Is it going against your dark side, huh? Well, look at me. I'm a goff. I dress in dark clothes but I'm still happy to be here.'

'Oh, that's what it is. I thought somefairy was dying or something,' His sneer turned into a grimace. Then he sighed. 'It's not the colours, it's the whole atmosphere. It just doesn't seem right.' He sniffed the air and looked around the room. 'I can sense it.'

'Well, her on the gate seemed fine, in a gate keepery sort of way,' I said chirpily.

'Yeah, but that woman in red, yeah – she wasn't right.' He picked at the sole of his shoe – then smelt his finger – yuk!

'Oh don't be stupid. It was just an old woman ...'

I didn't get time to finish as the lady on the desk beckoned us over. As we all stood up she quickly said, 'Just two of you will do.'

'Come on, Bess. We'll do the explaining.'

The lady smiled sweetly as we approached. 'So how can I help you?'

'Well, we're trying to find my sister, Bugface – I mean, Myrtle. She's kind of funny looking. Sort of skinny with red frizzy hair,' I said.

'And you'd like to see the reader?' she said.

'Yes, the old woman in the red hood said we could see her,' said Bessie.

'Well, the usual reader is off sick today but we have a supply in to cover but I have to say ... ' she leant forward across the desk, turning her head first left then right before continuing in a hushed voice, ' ... she's not the usual calibre of reader we get from the supply agency. She's been very impatient with the previous clients and ...'

I tried hard to listen as she rattled on but was

quickly distracted by an object on the shelf behind her. 'I'm so sorry,' I said, interrupting her. 'But who's that?' I pointed to a small silver framed picture of a young woman. She was smiling cheerfully.

'Oh, that's a picture of my sister. It was painted some time ago.'

'Crikey, Bess who does she look like?' Bessie shrugged her shoulders and pulled a 'no idea' face. 'Does she live here – with you?' I asked.

No, she died some time ago now.'

'Oh, I'm sorry. I didn't realise.' I felt a bit guilty for bringing up such bad memories for her.

'You weren't to know, were you? It was hard at first, what with the fairychids too … '

'Hell! You mean you brought them up alone – you're a martyr. Isn't she Bess? – a martyr!

'No …,' said the lady.

'You're far too modest …' I said butting in before she could finish.

'Oh for goodness sake! You're not listening. I didn't bring the fairychids up. I lost them too, just after Maud died.'

'Oh you poor thing – three deaths in a row. No wonder you're in such a state.' I patted her hand in a kind of comforting way.

She looked at me horrified. 'I beg your pardon.'

'… er, em,' I stuttered. 'I-I just mean when three fairies close to you die …'

'For your information the fairychids did not die ... they were taken – just two weeks after their mother's demise. They just vanished like a portal at sunrise – gone, never to be seen again.'

She buried her head deep into her hankie where she stayed for what seemed like an eternity.

'Get her out of that hankie, Aggie,' called Fred. 'Time's running out. We need to get going.'

'We can't just leave her, can we? I mean, she's all upset and that.'

She raised her head suddenly and let out a long pitiful wail. 'Those poor little chids. I wonder what happened to them. Such cute little faces and tiny little hands and feet. They were special. Their father wasn't from round here.'

'She was the same age as me – my twin.'

'and she had twins ...' said Bessie.

'Well, yes – that often happens.'

'and special powers ...' I said.

'Yes! I've told you all this.'

Bessie and I looked at each other but before we had time to share our thoughts, the old woman in the red hood emerged from the badly spelt poster door. She coughed loudly then cleared her throat as if ready to talk. 'Er, hem ... she'll see you now.' Her voice was low and deep. Most odd ...

'Come on, what're you waiting for?' Bessie pushed me towards the door which slowly creaked open as we approached.

'Crikey, it's a bit dark in here, isn't it? I can't see a bleeding thing!' I felt along the wall for a light switch.

'Er hem. Leave the light off. The reader needs to see your aura,' boomed the red hooded lady as she closed the door behind us. She moved to the front of the room and took her place behind a huge wooden table where the reader, dressed in a black hooded robe, was seated. Another red hooded old woman stood to the other side of her.

We moved nearer to the desk but were quickly stopped by the original woman. 'Er hem, no! STOP! Come no closer. The reader needs space to, er ... read.'

We backed away, finding the opposite end of the room where two seats awaited us.

The reader raised herself up from behind the desk. 'Er, hem ...' She coughed loudly, cleared her throat then spoke in a low menacing kind of voice. Her hood fell low over her face, covering her facial features entirely. 'I understand you have lost your sister.'

Grrr! Why does every being I meet jump to the same – wrong – conclusion! 'Not exactly lost, more sort of misplaced,' I said, huffily.

'Er hem ... and you want me to help you to find her?'

'Well, yes. That's why we're here,' I said, somewhat sarcastically.

'Er, hem … you weren't exactly nice to your sister when you had her, were you? Calling her Bugface all the time …'

'It was just a friendly nickname … Hang on, how do you know that?'

'Er, hem …well, er, I-I'm s-supposed to know everything!' She thumped her fist angrily on the table. 'Er, hem … I'm the reader.'

'Alright, alright. Keep your hood on.' I sat back, wearily.

'Er, hem … so do you want my help or not?'

Mmmm, do I want her help or not?

'Yes, she does!' said Bessie, seeing my delay in answering.

'Er, hem … so how do you intend to pay for such information?' said the reader.

'Well, I have a few credits …' I started counting on my fingers.

… 'Er, hem … I don't want your credits. I have something else in mind.'

'Which is?' I said.

'That bag on your back – what's in there?'

I tried to put the true contents out of my mind so she couldn't 'see' what was really in there. 'O-Oh nothing much. Just a few bits and pieces.' A slight panic came over me. Arty could pop up at any moment and I needed the bag with all the ransom items in it.

'Mmmm – I'll take it as payment,' said the reader, her hood flapping slightly as she spoke.

'But ...'

'I want it!' She yelled.

A loud cough came from one of the assistants which was duly ignored by the reader.

Still reeling from the shock of her demands, I tried to reason with her. 'But I need to keep the bag with me at all times. It's – er – sentimental value.'

'Er, hem ... Do you want to find your sister or not?' Her voice seemed to rattle with anger.

'Yes, of course.'

'Er, hem ... then the bag?'

'Okay, okay – you can have the bag.' I reluctantly handed it over to one of the assistants.

'Er, hem ... good! So have you brought me the ransom notes? I should be able to get a location from them.'

I turned quickly to Bessie. 'I wasn't even thinking about the ransom notes. How could she know that?'

'Er, doh! She's the reader, isn't she? Just give them to her and let's get out of here. This is freaking me out.'

'They're in here somewhere,' I said, rummaging through my pockets. I took care not to touch or think about the wooden whistle which was still tightly wrapped in its muslin jacket.

'Er, hem ... Do hurry, dearie.' The reader's voice became more sinister as her impatience brewed. 'I don't have all day.'

'Sorry ... Ah, here they are!' I held the papers triumphantly in my hand.

'Er, hem ... let me see,' said a hooded assistant, snatching one of the ransom notes from my hand and placing it face down in front of the reader.

'Give me ... er, hem ... Give me the all seeing veil of Walshong, Pet ...' she stopped mid word then continued, 'Er, please.'

A noise like a stifled snigger came from where the original hooded woman stood.

'What's going on here?' I said, jumping up from the chair. My wings twitched nervously – something just wasn't right here.

'SILENCE!' The reader lifted her head slightly, revealing a veiled face where only the top of her face was visible. 'Stay seated.'

She took the ransom note from the desk and slapped it to her forehead. It contorted heavily revealing a third eye which protruded just above two bushy eyebrows.

I forgot my suspicions and became totally absorbed in what I'd just seen. 'Yuk! That's just *so* gross it's actually cool,' I said to Bessie who was fanning herself with the other note from the kidnapper.

'Is it me or is it really hot in here?' Her face reddened and sweat beads began to form and glisten above her upper lip.

'Oh, for portals sake, Bess. It's only an extra eye,' I whispered casually as if this was a normal every day occurrence.

The reader rocked back and forth in her chair, groaning and sighing, the ransom note still stuck firmly to her forehead. She stopped suddenly then waved her arms around wildly in the air. 'Er, hem ... there she is! I see a young fairychid, sort of skinny with frizzy red hair.'

Okay, now tell me something I don't know!

'Er, hem ... she appears to be surrounded by creatures, strange creatures ...'

I leapt to my feet again. 'What kind of creatures – it can't be sprites, we've already ...'

'SILENCE!' screamed the reader, spreading her fingers out in front of her across the full depth of the desk. 'These creatures are grey not green ... and they smell ...'

I shuddered and wriggled noisily. 'Oh, hell – not moshtikes! I can't bear those bog dwellers. They slime all ...'

'NOT Moshtikes! These are grey, smell like sewers and have ...'

She didn't need to finish the sentence. It was now blatantly obvious which creatures she meant. I turned at once to Bessie, who had her hands tightly pressed against her pointy ears.

'Bloody marvellous!' I said. 'Grublins!'

'Ooommpphh,' sighed Bessie as she slipped off the chair and crashed straight onto the floor. Her head clipped the back of the wooden skirting board as she fell.

'Oh, crikey. Don't faint now, Bess,' I said, trying to haul her back up on the chair but she was a dead weight. From behind the desk the two hooded assistants stood and watched as I struggled. 'Well, give us a hand!'

The reader gestured to one of the red hooded women who, after pulling her hood down even further, drifted across the room to us. A flowery smell wafted around as she bent down to lift Bessie up. I sniffed the air. It was familiar in some way. 'Don't I know you?' I said, trying to get a better look inside the red hood.

The assistant shook her head, tugged on her hood then pulled on Bessie's arm to raise her up.

'It's just that your perfume reminds me of ...'

THUMP! The reader's fist hit the large table once more, directing my gaze away from the hooded woman who, I'm sure, sighed with relief.

'Go now,' she shouted. 'Er, hem ... the reading is ended.'

'What? That's it? Can't you tell us anything else?'

I said, struggling to my feet, one arm under Bessie's shoulder.

'Er, hem ... that's all you need to know. Grublin City is where you'll find your *lost* sister.' She waved us towards the door before adding, 'And thanks for the bag!'

The other assistant pushed open the door revealing Bessie's sorry state to all outside.

'What happened to her?' said Fred, jumping up to take Bessie's other arm.

'Oh, need you ask?' I said as we sat her in between us on one of the waiting room chairs.

'Not Grublins – in there?' Fred pointed to the door now slammed shut.

'No, not in there, you fool. Grublin City – that's where Myrtle's being held,' I said.

'I told you red for danger, didn't I?' said Gilbert, gloomily.

'Red indeed,' I said, completely ignoring him and addressing Fred. 'And you'll never guess what she took for payment?'

'Surprise me!' he said, pushing a slumping Bessie back into an upright position.

'Only my backpack! It had all the ransom bits in it. A bit odd, don't you think?'

He scratched his chinfluff then sniggered.

'How's that funny, Fred? We need that stuff for Arty!'

'You needed bits of bread and empty drink cartons to give to Arty, yeah?'

'You're not making any sense, Fred. You sure you didn't hit your head too!' I slapped the side of his head playfully.

'I swapped the bags, you twit. Didn't you notice it being lighter after we'd stopped to eat?'

'I just thought the stuff had shifted around a bit.' Relief flooded through me like a rolling river.

'What shifted?' slurred Bessie, stirring from her fainting fit and making a valiant attempt to sit upright.

'Wipe the dribble off your chin, Bess. It's really unappealing!' I propped her up again and watched as she used her sleeve to move the dribble around her face.

'What shifted?' she repeated. This time her eyes were open and the obvious signs of life were apparent although she was still a little shaky.

I explained what was said. 'I mean, why would she want my backpack? I hadn't thought about it at all so the only way she would know what was in it ...'

Fred cut in and quickly finished off my sentence. ' ... was if she *already* knew what was in there ...'

We sat for a while pondering over the question, racking our brains to find an answer. It wasn't until Gilbert commented once more on his red for danger theory that it finally struck me.

'How could we have been so stupid? Who else would make such demands like a spoilt chid?' I leapt up and ran across to the door with the badly spelt poster.

'What do you mean?' said Fred, following immediately behind.

'Gertie, bloody, Cruet!' I kicked open the door expecting to find 'the reader' and her two cronies but seeing the back door ajar, it was obvious that they'd already left.

'Hey, you can't do that?' cried the lady on the front desk.

'Well, where's the reader, huh?' I couldn't believe how angry I was. To be tricked was one thing but by Gertie Cruet, well that really made my wings flap!

She ran round from behind the desk to look inside the room for herself. 'She's probably out to lunch.'

'Oh, she's out to lunch alright!' I tapped my forefinger to the side of my head.

'Are you sure it was her?' said Fred. He walked around to the back of the huge wooden desk and started lifted pieces of paper up, searching for clues.

'Well, there was all the coughing and the low menacing voices,' I said, looking out the door for any signs of where they'd gone.

'And one of them giggled ...' added Bessie.

'And the flowery smell – it was violets. And who always wears violet perfume?'

'Violet Millett!' said Fred.

As we spoke, Gilbert fumbled around behind one of the chairs.

'Oi, what've you found?' asked Fred.

Gilbert turned and screeched. He had something strapped to his head. 'Arrgghh, look at my all seeing eye.'

'Great, just take it off. I feel a right idiot as it is. You don't have to rub it in!' I snatched the fake eye from his head and threw it out the back door.

'So Gertie's got something to do with Myrtle's kidnapping then?' said Bessie, tugging at my sleeve.

'Oh, Bess, keep up, will you? Yeah, she's definitely behind it and no doubt Arty's pulling her strings,' I said.

'But why? Why take Myrtle?' she looked puzzled, trying to understand the sick motive for kidnapping a young fairy such as Myrtle.

'To get back at Aggie, of course,' said Gilbert, sourly. 'That Gertie Cruet's been waiting for this for a long time – since the pilpblast.'

'Yeah, thanks for that. She's not too keen on you either, remember?' I flicked his ear with my thumb and finger but he continued regardless.

'And what was the last thing Arty said as they took him off to Mursham Marshes?'

'I think it was somewhere on the lines of 'I'll get you back for this, Lichen' … or thereabouts.' Fred dropped his head down, obviously embarrassed at what he'd just said.

'Yeah, that's about right,' said Gilbert, bleakly. 'Now they're going to lure you to Grublin City for a double revenge whammy!'

'Ah,' I said, swallowing hard as the reality of what this was all about suddenly hit me. 'But they don't know that we know what they're up to, do they? So we have the element of surprise, not them!'

'And so?' said Fred.

'And so ... we're off to see the Moshtikes.'

'But what about Grublin City? And besides ... you hate those slimey creatures.' Bessie shuddered and mopped her forehead.

'Yes, there is that ... but putting the hatred aside for just a moment or two, they're the only ones who just might be able to help us. Then we'll deal with the likes of Gertie Cruet!'

# Chapter Ten

With Bessie now fully recovered we headed for the door that led back to the hexagonal courtyard.

'What about those fairychids? Do you know where they might be?' called the lady behind the desk as we left.

Drat! I'd forgotten about that. 'Mmm, possibly. Follow us back through the gate. We *may* have a surprise for you.'

'D'you mean the twins, Aggie?' said Bessie somewhat excitedly. 'Could she really be their long lost auntie?'

'Not sure, besides I've got other things on my mind. Just bring her along in case.' When I'd first spoken to the lady I'd had all sorts of reunions going on in my head. Now the only reunion I wanted was with Gertie Cruet!

We turned the corner and headed towards the gate where the old lady gatekeeper was. She was leaning heavily against the white picket fence catching her breath. Her knitting lay in an untidy heap on the ground.

Bessie rushed to reach her. 'Are you okay? What happened?' She held the gatekeeper's arm gently.

'There were three of them,' she said shakily. 'I thought it was the reader until she threw her hood off. I couldn't read their thoughts, some kind of mind block. And that nasty spiteful face – I won't forget that for a long while.'

'Here, sit for a bit.' Bessie ushered her into the sentry box and sat her down. The gatekeeper took a deep breath and then continued. 'She wanted to know if you'd left anything out here. She just wanted something – anything that was yours.' This time she looked directly at me as she spoke. Her hand trembled as she reached out and grasped my arm tightly.

'B – But that's okay we didn't leave anything here,' I stuttered.

'Ah, but you did leave something out here, didn't you?' Her eyes strayed to the left.

I looked along the length of the white picket fence and back at her in dismay. 'The twins – where are the twins?'

'She took them. Her and her two helpers – they grabbed them and flew off in that direction,' she pointed towards the north. 'She said you'll know where to find them.'

'Bloody hell! – I wonder if she knows what they really are?'

'I don't think she does.' She took a sip of smint tea, poured from a metal flask by her side. 'They were still in fairy form when she took them.'

The poor lady from the red room was beside

herself with grief. 'Not again,' she cried. 'They're lost again.'

'Well, not *lost* exactly, just misplaced.' It was becoming a familiar answer of late. 'They might not even be the right ones – just lots of coincidences.'

'So much for the element of surprise. She must have realised that you'd sussed her out,' said Fred.

The lady from the red room blew her nose noisily into her hankerchief. I waited until it was firmly out of sight – I had a slight aversion to snotty hankies – then leant forward to talk to her. 'Look ...'

'Edie,' she said.

'Look, Edie. This is all my fault. She – Gertie – she's had it in for me since the pilpblast. It's a long story – which involves Gilbert quite a lot!' I added quickly.

'I'll show her ... ' he said.

'No, not now ...' Too late. Gilbert the smell appeared where Gilbert the fairy once stood. He wove himself in and out, spreading his revolting smell all over us and into every available orifice.

'Enough!' coughed Fred. 'We've got enough to contend with already. Change back – now!'

Gilbert's fairy features reappeared almost immediately except for his feet which took a little longer to materialise. 'I just wanted to show the lady.' He looked over at Edie who was as white as a clean pilp. 'I didn't mean to scare you,' he said apologetically.

'It's just that I've never seen anything like that before,' she said, bringing out the snotty hankie from her pocket once more and repeating the blowing nose process.

'Welcome to our world!' I said, throwing my arms up in the air.

'I have seen other things …,' she sniffed, 'but not like that.'

'What do you mean *other* things?' said Fred.

She tucked her hankie away in her pocket and straightened her skirt with her hands. 'Other things like … this!' She snapped her fingers and promptly disappeared.

'Mmmm, that could be useful,' I said.

'What do you mean that could be useful? The woman's just disappeared!' said Fred, brusquely.

Edie, still sniffing, reappeared at the end of the white fence – in the form of Gertie Cruet.

Even more useful!!

'Wow! How'd you do that?' cried Gilbert, running up to see her. 'That's brill. I want to do that too!'

'Oh, great! He's off again, never satisfied.'

'Er, more to the point, how *did* she do that?' said Bessie, following Gilbert to the end of the fence.

'Doh! She's a changeling, isn't she?' I called after her.

Edie AKA Gertie began to walk back to the wooden sentry box where Fred and I awaited her explanation but the old lady gatekeeper beat us to it. Readers, huh!

'But I never sensed the changeling in you, Edie.' She stood up and patted Edie's hand. 'You must have suppressed the urge to change for so many years.'

'When my sister died and I lost the twins, I vowed never to use the powers again. They seemed to bring nothing but trouble to my family – but I see now that they may be of some good after all.'

'Edie – do you think you could change back again? Looking at Gertie like this makes me feel *very* uncomfortable – and strangely angry!' I dug my fist deep into my pocket and fought to control the urge to thump the Gertie who stood before me. 'Phew! That's better,' I said as Edie changed back to her own body.

'Does this mean you're coming with us then?' said Gilbert, excitedly. 'Cos if you do, perhaps you can show me how you can appear in different places like that.' But before Edie had half a chance to answer, a large blue dragonfly, with a crumpled antennae, flew in front of her face before landing untidily on a fence post. It sat there for a while trying to catch its breath. It's large bulbous eyes nodding with each intake.

'It's one of ours – Old Growler.' I reached into the pouch that was strapped to the back of his abdomen and pulled out a roll of paper. 'It's from Pa – oh, no!'

'What? What's happened?' said Bessie.

'It's Albert,' I said. 'He's disappeared – not been seen for hours. They found his pilp sack on the other side but no trace of him.'

'You don't think …' Bessie feigned a swoon.

'What? I don't think Arty's anything to do with it? Well, doh – yes, I do!'

'But why? He's got Myrtle,' said Fred. 'What more does he want?'

I shook my head, 'I'm not sure but Pa needs me home straight away.'

'What about the Moshtikes?' said Gilbert. 'You said we were …'

'They'll have to wait,' I said.

We took off and headed back towards Pilpsville. Edie flew along side trying to make reassuring comments. I fingered the whistle in my pocket. Just one blow was all it needed. It could make everything alright again – for me. It felt smooth yet soft like velvet against my hand.

In my dreamlike state, I never noticed Edie fly up close to my ear. 'Get your hand off that whistle, Aggie Lichen,' she whispered gently.

I withdrew my hand angrily from my pocket and turned my face to hers. 'I was just … '

'Such a powerful weapon is so easy to sense. Keep it hidden. Best leave it there and thus avoid the dire consequences it may bring.' Edie patted my pocket and smiled. 'You're not the first to be lured by its song – just be sure you're not the last though.'

Her words swum around my head as we soared higher to catch the current, which would speed us on our way home. The east wind carried us quickly to our destination. Hardly a word was said for the whole return journey. Bessie could only manage 'Poor Albert, poor, poor Albert,' every 20 minutes or so. Fred and Gilbert just hung onto each other and flew silently behind.

As the sparkling silver roofs of Great Molaring appeared in our sights, we began our descent into Pilpsville. Over the three storey houses of Premolam, across the browner hues of Canningford until at last the well-worn streets of Insisorton lay beneath us. It had been an exhausting flight which had pushed our wings to the limit and sapped all our energy. I floated downwards and beckoned to the others to follow. We could walk the last few hundred metres and rest our aching wings. Landing near the pilp plant we shielded our eyes from the enormous mirrored windows which shone brightly. They caught the rays from the two suns and reflected back the light.

'What's going on?' said Edie as we got nearer.

A large crowd had gathered outside, shouting and pounding at the great wooden door. A few hovered over the huge windows, their faces pressed against the glass.

'This is the centre of our operations,' said Fred, grandly. 'The place where we get all our energy from, to light the streets. The place where magic dust for the pilp donors is extracted. The place where credits are given.'

'And it's shut?' questioned Edie, stopping directly across the street from the mob.

'Gertie Cruet's father runs it,' I said.

'Do you think he's still there?' asked Bessie.

'I doubt it. Gertie would have sent a message to let him know we'd found her out,' I said.

'Look, there's a note pinned to the door,' said Fred, running over and pushing his way through the throng of fairies which now stood five deep.

We carried on walking, quickening the pace with each step. 'Catch us up, Fred,' I called. 'I need to get home.'

As we turned into my road, the familiar sight of my house fell upon my eyes. I had spent so little time there lately I'd quite forgotten how brown and ugly it really was. Still, it did have a shed! Ma stood on the doorstep and on seeing me, ran down to greet us.

'Where've you been? I sent Old Growler ages ago.' She hugged me tightly then turned and faced the others. 'I've been going out of my mind with worry about Albert and Myrtle, and now they say it's all kicking off at the pilp plant.'

As if on cue, Fred flew up behind us. He puffed and panted as he drew his breath. 'The note says he's been called away on urgent family business – doesn't say when he'll be back!'

'Doesn't say *if* he'll be back, more like!' said Bessie sarcastically.

'So that's why we've had no power!' said Ma. 'Goodness knows what we'll do now.'

'Oh it's okay,' said Fred. 'Mr Fettock's sorted out a replacement – just until things are sorted.'

Trust old Fettock to get his nose in. Up to that point I'd forgotten all about him – and school.

'Well I suppose that's something!' said Ma, brushing down her apron. 'Right, you'd all better come inside quickly. Tell me and Pa all you know then we'll fill you in about Ferrett.' Ma grasped my hand tightly, 'And bring your new friend. I've a feeling she fits somewhere into this horrendous jigsaw too.'

Edie smiled at Ma. They were of a similar age and she seemed to warm to Ma quickly.

'You're a changeling, aren't you?' said Ma, as we went inside the house. 'I can tell from your eyes. They can't seem to stay the same colour, can they?'

She ushered Edie into the kitchen and pulled out a chair for her.

'I'm sorry,' sighed Edie. 'I've only just started using

my powers again. I haven't quite got the eyes under control.'

Pa walked in, having heard the conversation from the sitting room and stared hard and long at Edie. 'When they're blue they remind me of two other little changelings we know – where *are* Stan and Alf?'

Edie was now unable to control her tears as well as her eye colour. She burst out crying, wiping the rivers of salt water that formed away with the hankie retrieved once more from her pocket. Yuk!

Ma, also unable to affect any control over her tear ducts, joined in. It was left to Pa to sit and listen as one by one we relayed the dreadful events and their possible consequences on the fairy world.

'But you haven't blown the whistle yet,' he whispered, turning his head to me so the others couldn't hear.

'No,' I murmured. 'But it tried hard to tempt me, Pa. It calls to me all the time. I'll be glad to be shot of it.'

He smiled briefly before resuming the conversation with the others. 'So that Gertie Cruet's got our Myrtle, huh?'

'And the twins,' said Gilbert.

'Yes,' said Pa, 'and the twins. And you think Wilfred Cruet has gone to join Gertie in Grublin City?'

'Possibly but forget him – what of Albert?' I said.

Pa told us how Albert had gone out on the

nightsgritch with a couple of friends from school. They said they lost him near the blue house with the wishing well. They turned round and he'd disappeared. His pilp sack was found hanging on a branch nearby.'

Ma howled loudly. This time it was Edie's turn to join in. 'Poor Albert, poor Myrtle, poor twins!' she cried.

'That's the house where the sick pilp donor was, wasn't it, Aggie?' said Bessie, speaking loudly over the constant sobbing. 'The one who dressed them up as squiggles ...' She stopped suddenly, realising at once that she'd said more than she should have and backtracked.

'Yes, she dressed her pets up as squiggles, didn't she?' Bessie blushed and looked around for support. With donor interaction strictly forbidden, we all nodded frantically for fear of being caught out. Phew! I pressed my finger quietly to my lips as I looked over at Bessie's bright red face. Better if I did the talking!

'So what do we do first, Pa? Myrtle or Albert?'

'and the twins,' sobbed Edie.

'It might be best if you split into two groups.'

'Me and Fred ...' I began.

'No,' chipped in Pa. 'I was thinking more of you and Gilbert! Fred could make his way to Grublin City, taking Edie with him.'

'What about me?' said Bessie. 'I'm brave and have my uses!'

'Not where the Grublins are concerned though, huh!' Pa laughed as Bessie shuddered. 'Probably best if you go with Aggie and Gilbert. I only wish I could go with you myself. I feel pretty useless staying here and waiting for news.' He rubbed his shrivelled wing, cursing loudly as he did so.

'It's fine, Mr Lichen,' said Fred. 'We're happy to help, aren't we Gilbert?'

Gilbert's pleasure at being teamed with me and Bess was shown instantly – in the form of his alter ego, the revolting smell.

'It'll come in useful – I'm sure,' grinned Fred, awkwardly.

'What about the Moshtikes, Pa? They're our only way of getting Myrtle back in one piece,' I said.

This time it was Pa who shuddered. 'Let's find Albert first. Then, if Fred and Edie let us know what's going on with the Grublins, we'll be in a better position to approach the Moshtikes.'

Edie blew her nose loudly into her snotty hankie then stood up. 'So are we ready to go?' She wobbled slightly and had to steady herself by holding onto a chair.

'No fairy – or – changeling is going anywhere until they've had something to eat and drink. And no doubt you could all do with a quick sit down.' Ma took Edie's hand and helped sit her back on the chair again.

'But Albert ... Myrtle ...' I said.

'You'll be of no use to either if you haven't got the energy to fly and besides ... Pa still has to tell you the news about Ferrett.'

Ma handed round cups of smint tea and a plate of rose petal cakes she'd baked earlier. In troubled times, Ma always baked, and although these examples were terribly under cooked, they were gratefully eaten by all.

'So,' said Pa, 'to Ferrett.' He sat himself down and looked around the room. His face frowned deeply showing the creased lines that were becoming more apparent with each adventure we had. 'He's disappeared too – just before Albert. His house has been shut up, shutters closed, curtains drawn and him, nowhere to be found.'

'Perhaps ...,' I coughed, spitting pieces of cake across the table as I spoke, 'Perhaps he's just gone visiting. He's got lots of rich relatives to stay with all over Mirvellon.'

'But he's our oldest friend. Surely he'd have said something to us,' said Pa. 'He's always around to support the family when we have a problem.'

'Maybe he just got sick of your problems,' said Gilbert, reverting back to fairy form once more. 'He's probably gone off on holiday.'

'Crocks – you're really rather a rude little fairy, aren't you Gilbert Trickle?' said Ma.

'I'm sorry,' said Fred, giving his little brother a deep and dangerous stare. 'He seems to have got worse since the incident with 'he who must not be mentioned' in Spercham.'

'Well, all that aside, Ferrett's gone, Cruet's gone and Albert's disappeared. All pretty strange, huh Aggie?' Pa looked at me as if I had the answers curled up tightly in my grubby little hand ready to read out at a seconds notice. For a moment I just stared back. How the tides had changed. One minute I was the Aggie Lichen who can't seem to do a thing right and the next I am the Aggie Lichen everyone relies upon to solve their problems. No wonder we teenagers are confused – we don't know who we are!

'Huh, Aggie,' repeated Pa, breaking my stare.

'Er, yeah – pretty strange.' I munched on another rose petal cake and slurped down the last of my smint tea noisily. 'If we're all done,' I said wiping the crumbs away from my mouth with the side of my hand. 'Best we all get going.'

Ma packed another bag of goodies for me. Bessie and Gilbert then filled a smaller bag for Edie and Fred.

'It'll keep you going for a bit,' she said passing the bags over. 'Aggie, I know it's Albert you're looking for but please don't be out all night. You don't seem to have had a moments rest since this whole thing started.' She gave me a tight squeeze and kissed me lightly on the head. 'Thank you Bessie, and you Gilbert. We do appreciate your help too.'

Gilbert scowled then muttered, rather loudly, under his breath, 'I'd rather be going to Grublin City. I'd sort that Gertie Cruet out once and for all!'

'Which is precisely why you need to go with Aggie,' said Fred. 'If you come with me you'll go rushing in without thinking and then we might never get Myrtle back. No, go with Aggie and Bess, and use that smell to your advantage.' He leant over and gave his sibling a small hug from which Gilbert pulled away.

'Let us know how you get on Fred,' I said, 'I'll keep my aerial tuned in to your frequency.'

'Be careful.' His hand brushed against my hand as he passed by to leave. 'And don't take any risks,' he added as he shut the front door behind him.

Outside the light was failing as another night drew slowly in. Another night without Myrtle and now without Albert. We set off towards the portal knowing that at any moment the suns' rays would die and the route to the other side would be revealed. Passing over town we saw that the angry crowd outside the pilp plant had dispersed. Many of them would no doubt be on the nightsgritch – and be left wondering what exactly to do with the pilps they collected. Without an expert running the pilp plant, and

Wilfred Cruet was really the only expert, the consequences could be awful. But I'd greater things on my mind and as we swooped down to pass through to the human world I wondered exactly what we'd find.

# Chapter Eleven

'Is this the place?' said Gilbert, landing heavily on the window sill of the house. 'Cos if it is, I'll smell them all out and find Albert.'

'Calm down, will you?' I said, fluttering down beside him. I pulled him roughly towards me and pushed my face into his. 'We're not even sure if he's in there, are we? Pa just said he was last seen here so just wait before you do anything – stupid!'

'And if he was in there, he'd have the pilp sack with him, wouldn't he?' said Bessie, sidestepping the crusty remains of a bird pecked snail as she spoke.

'First, let's just have a scout around and see if there's any other evidence,' I said.

'And then we'll smell them out!' said Gilbert, gleefully rubbing his hands together.

'Yes, Gilbert! *Then* we'll give them a smell to remember. What d'you reckon, Bess?' I turned to where she'd just been standing, hoping for her agreement. But she'd moved in closer to the pilp donor's window. She just stood staring into the window of the house.

'Bess? You okay? What's wrong? Why are you staring like that?' I grabbed her shoulder.

'It's Albert ...' she said.

'I know,' I patted her back gently, trying to reassure her. 'We'll find him. He's probably off inventing something ...'

'No,' she pointed at the window. 'It's Albert, he's in there – in there ... talking to a pilp donor!'

Gilbert and I threw ourselves at the window in horror. Our faces pressed against the coldness of the glass, the quickness of our breath causing misty patches on the panes.

'What the hell's he doing?' I said squishing my nose in closer. The chill of the glass rushing through my body made me shiver.

'Is *he* talking to the donor? Oh, that's not allowed!' Gilbert rubbed the window to have a clearer view. 'He's going to be in so much tr...'

I gave him a hefty shove – so hard that he almost fell off the ledge. 'Just shut up, will you? I'm trying to concentrate.' I screwed my eyes up tightly to get a better look, focusing in on the pilp donor's lips.

Gilbert edged cautiously to my left side. 'I just meant,' he whispered, 'that if someone told of him, then he'd be in trouble.'

'So don't tell!' spat Bessie as quietly as she could manage. 'Now let Aggie concentrate on reading the donor's lips.'

I watched carefully as the donor spoke to Albert. I couldn't believe what I was reading. I spelt the word out. 'K-i-d-n-a-p-p-e-d! He's only telling it about

Myrtle being taken. What an idiot! He's giving us all away.'

'Storm!' cried Bessie.

'A weather report, now of all times, Bess! How useful!'

'No – storm him. Let's go in there and whiz him out – like storm troopers.'

'Not that old myth again! You listen to such rubbish.' I scoffed. I patted my pocket, feeling the outline of the wooden whistle against my hand. I felt myself blush but I *had* to keep it secret – even from my best friend. But her suggestion made me think. 'You're absolutely right, Bess.'

'I am?' she said in surprise.

'Yes, and we've got our own storm trooper right here – or should I say smell trooper!' I grabbed Gilbert roughly by the collar.

'Gerroff!' he shrieked, struggling fiercely to get out of my grip. 'You're strangling me!'

I loosened my grip and turned him round to face me. Couching down to his level, I proceeded to give him his secret mission. 'You are to change into smell mode, slip through the gap, stink the place out and return to this window sill with Albert, understand?'

'You don't have to be so rough!' he said, rubbing his throat where he'd been 'strangled'.

'I said do you understand?' I pushed my face further into his.

'Yes, stop going on will you? Smell mode, gap, stink and Albert – yeah, I've got it.'

'And hurry up, we've still got the twins and Myrtle to find ...,' I said. But before I could finish the sentence he'd slipped into his alter ego, the smell. He slid silently through the window gap, curling and twisting up and down before heading towards the unsuspecting donor who still had its back to us. We watched with baited breath as the greeny-yellow smell whirled round and round, spreading its revolting stench thick and fast. It wasn't long before Albert and the donor stopped talking and reached for their noses, pinching the nostrils tightly together.

'I think Albert knows we're here!' I said, nudging Bessie in the ribs but she was too busy fussing with her hair to take any notice. 'I don't know why you bother with him. He's more interested in his flipping inventions than you.'

'Yeah,' she said dreamily. 'I know.'

It was like talking to a glass window pane and just as transparent as her feelings for my brother. Yuk!

A sudden and rapid tap from inside the donor's window startled the both of us. 'What the bloody hell is that?' I cried.

It was Albert. He was grinning – grinning in a scary fairy way. 'Come on in. Come and meet Martha.' He pointed to the donor who waved enthusiastically at the two of us. Its long blond hair bounced with every arm wave and the blueness of its eyes was dazzling.

I pulled Bessie quickly to the side of the window. We held onto each other tightly, carefully balancing on the edge of the battered sill, just out of sight of tapping Albert.

Although we couldn't see him, we could still hear his constant knocking and his voice calling us, 'Come on – come and meet her. Don't be scared!' he said.

'Oh my portals,' said Bessie, peering gingerly round the edge of the window. 'He's been hippermatised!' Her face was white with shock.

'I think you mean hypnotised!' I said, for once knowing what the correct word should be. I'd at least been awake in *that* lesson.

She turned back, her face deadly serious, 'We've got to get him out of there, Aggie. We've got to … aarrgghh!'

'Hello, you two.' Albert's head appeared suddenly round the window. 'You're not hiding from us are you?'

I grabbed his collar, pulling him out of the house and up close to me. 'What's the matter with you?' I whispered. 'You know we're not allowed to interact with the donors.'

'This is different.' He yanked my arm off of his. 'She's not like the other donors.'

'Oh, so now it's a she – not simply a donor!' I screamed. 'Crikey, Albert – our little sister is somewhere in Grublin City at the mercy of Arty Granger and Gertie Cruet and you're messing around with a ...'

'Oh, just listen will you?' It was his turn to pull my collar. 'She used to be a pilp collector – like us!'

My mouth dropped open and it took a while for my brain to engage again. 'Don't be ridiculous! That's impossible. It just can't happen ...'

'You're either a fairy or a human – or a Grublin,' Bessie shuddered, '- not both, Albert!'

'Come in and talk to her. She'll tell you how it happened ...'

'No, Albert. This is strictly forbidden.' The serious side in me came out now. This was such a bad move. 'Just blow the magic dust in its face and it'll forget about all of this ...'

'But that's how she remembered!' He threw his arms up in an exasperated manner. 'I blew the magic dust in her face when she spotted me but instead of making her forget, it made her remember – remember being a pilp collector.'

'Ah – but what if it's all a lie? What if it's a trap?' I looked around cautiously. I didn't trust humans at all. From the little I could see of their world, there wasn't much they wouldn't do to get what they wanted.

'I've been here for two days. I'm fine.'

'So why didn't you send an aerial message to let us know?' I said, deeply suspicious and leaning heavily towards Bessie's hypnotism theory.

'I just couldn't get a signal – that's all! Look, nothing's happened to me.' He spun around flying just a little way from the ground.

'Right, nothing 'cept the hippnatisation!' said Bessie crossly. She eyed the pilp donor through the window, looking her up and down, her upper lip curled in a sneeringly jealous manner.

'Oh, for portals sake! I've not been hypnotised and I'm under no spell. Just come and see for yourself.' Albert beckoned us through the gap in the window frame.

But Bessie and I remained rooted to the window sill. This was far too risky. Too much was at stake, leaving me no choice but to call for reinforcements. 'I'm sorry Albert,' I said in a commanding tone, patting the muslin covered package in my pocket. 'but I'm going to have to call for the storm ...'

He quickly interrupted me with a surprising but convincing statement. 'She knows Ferrett ... and Arty!'

Bessie and I looked at one another. 'Everyfairy knows Ferrett ...,' said Bessie.

'Exactly my point! Everyfairy – she *was* a fairy, a tooth fairy just like us.' Albert turned to the window and stared in at Martha. 'It's a terrible tale but you have to hear it for yourselves. Come on, slip through the gap.' He pointed to the rotted window frame, reaching out to help us through.

'Okay, but this had better be good!' I allowed myself to be pulled through the other side. The warmth of the room hit me full on making me gasp and catch my breath. Bessie followed, cautiously sidling up to me, her eyes widening as the towering figure of the pilp donor walked towards us.

'Hello,' she said quietly. 'I'm Martha. Please don't be frightened. I wouldn't hurt one of my own kind for all the tea in Pilpsville.'

She sat down on the floor in front of the window. Albert fluttered down and rested on her knee. 'Come on, Aggie. Surely you're not scared? Just listen to what Martha has to say.'

I stroked the lump in my pocket. Was this the emergency Pa had spoke about? Was this the time?

'Come on, Aggie,' whispered Bessie, 'I'll go if you go.' She looked at me briefly before gently flapping her wings together and swooping lightly down to Albert. I followed reluctantly, unsure of the whole situation.

'I'll just stay here,' I said, landing on a nearby book. I brought myself up to my full sixteen centimetres and said, 'So what's all this about, huh?' There was a slight quiver in my voice as I fought gallantly against my fears.

Martha spoke in a low, gentle voice. 'I was born in Pilpsville many years ago ...'

'But you're only about seven years old!' I cut in quickly, sensing a flaw in her story.

'Stop interrupting!' said Bessie, obviously desperate to hear the tale. 'Let her tell the story.'

I shut up and adopted an 'I'm listening but there's a strong chance I may interrupt' pose.

Martha continued. 'In this human form I am the age of seven but in fairy years I would be ...' she touched her fingers, counting in sevens. 'I'd be around forty-nine now.' She moved the back of her hand across her eyes which glistened with the moisture of her tears.

'But how can that be? How did you end up here ... as a donor?' asked Bessie.

'Ferrett! He did it. He changed her.' Gilbert stepped from behind a jewellery box on the dressing table. Tiny specks of yellowy-green dust leapt off his clothing as he flew down to join us.

'Where have you been?' I growled. As part of a secret mission he'd been completely useless.

'I had a little bit of trouble changing back,' he groaned. 'But I could still hear what was going on – that Ferrett ...'

'Let Martha tell it, smelly!' said Albert, waving his hand in front of his nose. The smell was awful.

Martha stood up and opened the window slightly allowing fresh cold air to waft in and the dreadful smell to waft out!

'Gilbert's right,' she said sadly. 'This was Ferrett's doing. We were close when we were younger, very close.'

'Just how 'very close' do you mean?' I said suspiciously.

'She looked at her feet and swallowed hard. 'We were ... married.'

My mouth dropped open – as did Bessie's!

'That's not all.' Martha rose slowly to her feet, her head hanging low as she paced up and down the room. She bit her lip nervously as she walked.

Minutes of silence passed as we prepared ourselves for her next revelation. Impatient as ever, Bessie couldn't hold her tongue any longer. 'What's not all? Come on, tell us!'

She stuttered and stumbled as she fought against revealing the ultimate surprise. Beads of sweat formed on her brow as she took a deep breath and prepared to spit out the truth. 'We – We had ... a son.'

'What? Is that it? You had a son!' I fluttered upwards towards the gap in the window, the only way out. 'Well if that's the best you can ...'

She cut in quickly. 'His name was ... Arthur.'

'Huh?' This meant nothing to me.

She sighed as if wanting the moment to end quickly but still seemed reluctant to part with the news and the consequences of what she might say. 'His name was often shortened though – to ...'

Then my brain finally clicked into action. 'Arty! Oh my portals. You're Arty Granger's mother!'

Martha sank to her knees and sobbed uncontrollably into her hands.

'Arty Granger had a mother! Bloody hell!' Bessie leant back and promptly fell off the book she'd been sitting on.

'Aggie,' whispered Albert, wagging his finger, 'Go on, Aggie.' He pointed to Martha who was still weeping heavily.

'Er, no,' I whispered, 'I don't do comfort very well – Bess, go and sort Martha out will you?'

Bessie was quite at ease comforting Martha although she could do little except pat her on the shoulder. She slapped her tiny hand against Martha's skin. It made little impact but the gesture made Martha's mouth turn up slightly in the form of an almost smile.

'He was only after my money. As soon as young Arthur was born he wanted rid of me.'

'But how? How'd he do it?' I asked.

'He went to the lowest possible place – Grublin City. There he found a Grublin Grolsher, the Grublin equivalent of our healer except they're evil to the core.'

Unsurprisingly, at the mention of the word Grublin, Bessie began to hyperventilate. I pulled a crispy brown bag from my pocket and threw it in her direction.

'Yeah,' I said. 'Carry on.'

'What about your friend?' said Martha, concern apparent in her voice.

I waved my hand towards the puffing figure of Bessie. 'Oh, she'll be fine. It's just her Grublin phobia,' I said offhandedly. 'Now ... as you were saying.'

'Well, he got them to make up a vanquishing potion, you know, to vanquish the pilp collector in me.' She dabbed her eyes before continuing. 'He wanted me away from Mirvellon – and Arty – forever.'

'So why didn't he just kill you?' Albert flicked Gilbert's ear. 'Ouch, what'ja go and do that for?'

Bessie gave Gilbert a stern look but that didn't deter Gilbert one bit. He rubbed his ear then spoke again. 'If he wanted you gone for good, he'd have had you done in, wouldn't he?

'You'll have to excuse him,' said Albert, kicking Gilbert in the calf. 'He's a little short on tact at the best of times!'

'No, he's right. I often wonder about that myself.' She looked straight at Gilbert as if trying to reason with him. 'Perhaps he just couldn't live with my death on his hands.'

There was a pause in the conversation as we all took time to think but Gilbert's patience was wearing thin and he was the first to break the cold chill that filled the air.

'So what are we gonna do?' he said, flying round and round Martha's head like an irritating bluebottle. She pretended to try and swat him. He came to rest on the window ledge then asked the same question I was thinking. 'We change her back.'

'And how d'you plan to do that, huh?' said Albert.

I patted my pocket. Was this the time? Was this the emergency? I mulled it over and over in my head as the others talked. I still didn't know if I believed her story. It just seemed too weird to be true.

'Perhaps we could go and talk to the Grublin Grolsher,' said Gilbert, pulling Grublin style faces each time he passed Bessie.

'Er, no.' said Martha. 'Too dangerous and he's probably long dead by now. Perhaps there's another way?'

Bessie flew up sharply, looking pleased with herself. 'I know – what if we go to the healers?'

'Well, no. They probably won't believe me.' She twisted the hem of her nightie. 'Perhaps there's another way?'

'Okay, stop.' I'd heard enough and had made my decision. 'I think I *may* have a way of fixing this.' I said cautiously.

'*You* do?' said Gilbert, disbelievingly. His face creased up as he squinted heavily through his glasses.

'W-Well, yeah. At least I think so.' I dug deep into my pocket, stroking the softness of the wood as it caught my fingers. As the others crowded round, I took out the secret object that had been occupying so much of my thoughts. Martha knelt down then pushed her face in close to my hand.

'Hold on,' she said. 'It's too small for me to see'. She ran to a drawer returning quickly with a hand held enlarger. She leant down pressing the lens to her eye. 'Oh wow! Is that what I hope – think – it is?'

'What? What the hell is it?' cried Albert.

At first I hesitated, realising how my reply would be received. Then I took a breath and just spat it out. 'It's a whistle – a storm trooper whistle.' I said trying to justify the pathetic excuse for a piece of wood that lay openly in my hands. The peeling varnish broke away with every touch of my finger.

'You said there was no such thing, Aggie Lichen,' said Bessie in her best scolding voice.

'I couldn't say,' I said, remembering my promise to Pa.

'Well, what are you waiting for? Blow it then,' said Albert scornfully. 'Come on, let's see what happens! Storm troopers indeed!'

I thought carefully for a minute about the 'dire

consequences'. But then, seeing as I didn't really believe in it anyway, sucked in a long deep lungful of air then blew with all the power I could find – nothing! I tried again – and again – and again. The silence of their stares cut through me like broken glass.

'Oh, give over will you. Blame Pa. He's the believer not me,' I said almost apologetically.

'But you blew on it so you must believe too!' sneered Gilbert.

'Try it again, please!' said Martha, desperately. 'My – er – mother told me tales of the storm troopers when I was a fairychid. Keep blowing, it's my only hope.'

I blew again and again and again but nothing happened.

Martha slumped down beside her bed and began picking threads from the hem of her nightie.

'Don't worry, we'll think of something else,' said Bessie.

'No,' said Martha, wiping away yet another tear from her swollen eyes. 'It's best that you just blow some magic dust in my face so I can forget everything all over again.'

Being the unsympathetic type, half of me wished Albert *would* just blow the bloody dust in her face – or at least pass me the pouch so I could do it! There was only so much whinging and whining a fairy could take! Besides, we'd found Albert and we now needed to meet up with Edie and Fred to rescue Myrtle.

'Perhaps she's right, Albert,' I said thoughtlessly. 'Put her out of her misery and blow the dust! We're wasting time here. We need to get to Myrtle.'

'How can you say that?' he said, crossly.

Easily, I thought – very easily. My sister was surely more important than this whinging pilp donor – come pilp collector!

'I just thought I might be able to persuade Arty – my son – to give up Myrtle to you ...,' wept Martha.

'Well, that's all well and good,' I said, unrepentantly. 'But we've still no way of changing you back and time's a wasting ... ' As I spoke I fluttered backwards towards the window landing gently on the ledge. The cold breeze from outside caught my wings blowing me upwards and into something soft.

'Ooopps – what was that?' I said turning round.

'Er hem! *Wheeze,* I'm sorry to interrupt, *wheeze,* but ...'

There in front of me were three over-weight, over-sixtyish and out of breath fairies. From the look of their tatty red suits, complete with threadbare silver capes, they'd worn the same clothing for many years. The heavy metal buckle on their belts, which fought against gravity to hold in their bulging stomachs, was the only give away to their true identities – S. T.

'S.T.? Ah, Storm Troopers! Ah ha! It's them!' I cried.

'It's what?' Albert swung around and faced the window. 'Bloody hell, it's them!'

Martha sat stunned on the floor. Gilbert and Bessie buzzed around her head dementedly.

'*Wheeze,* someone whistled?' said the smaller one.

'Well, yeah, but we whistled for the storm troopers – the finest, most courageous rescuers in all of Mirvellon!' I said sarcastically, looking the trio up and down in disbelief.

'And that's what, *wheeze,* you've got. Now, *wheeze,* what's the problem?'

'Martha crawled forward towards the window. Her eyes shone, full of hope. 'Can you turn me back into a pilp collector, can you?'

With his breathing now under control the smaller one scratched his bulging stomach then called to the larger fairy. 'Hmmm, possibly.' He turned to the rest of us. 'We do need proof that she was actually a pilp collector. What do you have?'

Albert took great pains to explain Martha's predicament at great length, only stopping when the smaller storm trooper put his hand up to stop him. 'Ted, do we have any gnat's milk?'

Ted looked through the small bag slung across his shoulder. 'Just a bit, Ern.' He threw the bottle to Ern who tipped the contents into a small cup. Martha reached out her hand eagerly. 'Oh, it's not finished yet.' He turned and looked at the other storm trooper. 'Pass me the purified dragonfly spit, Reg.'

After digging around a bit, Reg pulled out a small jar and passed it to Ted who dribbled a few drops of spit into the cup. Martha looked on, her eyes sparkling in anticipation.

'How much longer?' Her voice had a slight growling tone to it. I put it down to her impatience.

'I just need to add one more thing,' said Ted, fishing around in his pocket for the final ingredient. He sprinkled a brown sparkly powder into the cup then stirred it with his finger. 'There, that should do it. Just drink ...' Before he'd finished, Martha had snatched the cup between her forefinger and thumb and swallowed the contents.

'She's just a little eager to be re-united with her son,' said Albert apologising for her bad manners.

Gilbert, now perched on Martha's shoulder, called across to Ted. 'Nothing's happening! Why isn't she changing?'

Ted looked at his watch. 'Just give it around thirty seconds and it'll start. You might want to come and stand on the ledge – things could get *very* ugly!'

Taking Ted's advice the others quickly flew up and joined me on the ledge.

Ted tapped his watch. 'Shield your eyes – now!'

The episode that followed was something none of us would ever forget in a hurry. It all started quite innocently with a stunning explosion of light which spurted out of Martha's gaping mouth and ears. This was followed by a gentle popping sound as she began to shrink down to fairy size. But then the *ugly* part began as parts of her body went into horrific spasms resulting in various limbs becoming enlarged and contorted. Her ears grew longer and redder as they took on the pointed features of a true pilp collector.

It was just at that point that a sudden bang on the door made us all jump and diverted our attention away from the show. It was Martha's parents.

'Martha, are you okay?' came a voice strewn with panic. 'Open the door, sweetie.' Frantic twisting and rattling of the door knob followed.

Sensing trouble, Reg, Ted and Ern quickly flew over to the door and positioned themselves just above the keyhole. 'Just blow it through, Ern,' said Ted, passing him a large handful of magic dust. The sneezing fit that followed indicated that Ern had been successful and seconds later the sounds of footsteps retreating could be heard.

With all eyes back on the show, the most horrendous of all acts now followed. Martha, now crouched with her knees tucked under her, squealed as her back bent and twisted. Her newly formed wings emerged from between her shoulder blades glistening with beads of sweat. Lifting her head, she clenched her teeth together as she took control of them, spreading the membrane out wide to dry.

Ted tapped my arm. 'We've got to go now!' He beckoned to Reg and Ern who fluttered at once to his side. 'We've been whistled!'

'What about her?' I pointed to Martha who was struggling to get to her feet.

'Oh, she'll be fine in a minute or two. It's just like riding a dragonfly, when you've done it once you always remember what to do.'

Martha threw him an exasperated look as she fought to balance herself against the added weight of her newly formed wings.

'Now remember, if you need us again, whistle. Just allow us a little extra time to get to you before you blow – repeatedly!'

'Is that it? What about the dire consequences?' I said nervously.

'Oh, they're a different department altogether. But they'll be along later,' said Reg.

Very reassuring, I thought.

As the Storm Troopers disappeared through the window gap, Martha spoke her first words since being turned back. 'Oh my portals, how old were they?'

'I think you mean, thank you very much for

turning me back!' I said, crossly. 'After all, if it wasn't for my whistle …'

She straightened out her dress and shook her wings. 'I'm grateful, honest.'

Hmmm, she didn't sound it!

As she fluttered up clumsily to the window ledge I came face to face with her for the first time. The facial features Arty bore were now blatantly apparent in his mother as she stood before me. For an older fairy, she had still retained much of her youthful looks. Perhaps being a human for so many years had had some advantages.

'So – shall we go?' she said, flapping her wings gently back and forth.

'Yeah!' said Gilbert, eagerly. 'I can't wait to see the look on Arty's face when he sees you.'

Martha flew towards the gap before muttering her reply. 'Neither can I, Gilbert. Neither can I!'

# Chapter Twelve

'It's hardly changed at all,' remarked Martha as we emerged through the exit into Mirvellon. A cool breeze swept through the night sky.

'Perhaps you'd like to stop off at my house to freshen up,' said Bessie. 'It's not too far.'

'Er, no. It's probably best if I go straight to Grublin City and talk to Arty. After all, we don't want this terrible situation to go on any longer than necessary, do we?'

'No, of course not,' said Bessie, trying hard to hide her disappointment.

'It's going to be a little awkward getting through Pilpsville, though,' said Martha. 'I mean, Arty's mother is not exactly going to be popular, is she? Perhaps, Bessie, you could loan me your cardigan. And Albert, could I borrow your sunblockers? I'll give them back, honest!'

With Martha suitably disguised we headed for Pilpsville. Cutting through Insisorton would be the quickest route, flying high to avoid unnecessary stares from passersby.

'Ah, the pilp plant,' she said as we passed over the centrally located building. Its vast mirrored windows caught our reflections as we flew by. 'Does Wilfred Cruet still run it?'

'Up 'til a few days ago, yes. But he's disappeared – possibly gone to join his daughter, Gertie, in Grublin City,' said Albert.

'Gertie, huh? What's she like?'

'Oh, don't get me started on her!' I said. But before I could get started on her, a strange noise distracted me. 'Hey, what's that buzzing sound?'

'It's your aerial, idiot,' sneered Gilbert, taking great delight in my stupidness.

News, at last, from Fred and Edie. I tweaked the tip of my wing, after flicking Gilbert's ear first of course, and listened in. It was Fred.

'Lots of activity here but no sign of Myrtle or the twins. Grublins keep talking about Arty but he doesn't seem to be around. Deliveries of something or other keep coming in. They're definitely up to no good! Meet us just beyond the gnarled old tree outside the city gates. Ooops! Got to go – Grublins approaching.'

'Fred, Fred!' I shouted into the wing tip.

'He's gone, you fool!' muttered Gilbert.

This time it was Bessie who flicked his ear but only just before he turned himself into his smelly form.

'Oh, you little sod!' she said, taking a swipe at the yellowy wisp.

'Well,' I said, trying to ignore Gilbert's foul play. 'At least we know they're safe. We'll be with them in no time.'

Up ahead the silver roofs of Great Molaring sparkled in the moonlight. They shone like beacons as if to warn of the evil that lay beyond the towns border – Grublin City!

'It might be best if I go on alone,' said Martha suddenly as we swept over the wealthy town of Premolam. Their three storey buildings stood high and proud against the sky.

'What? Are you mad?' I said. Unbelievable! I'm waiting for the backlash of blowing the whistle – also known as dire consequences – and she wants to slope off on her own!

'I can reason with him – tell him to let Myrtle go.'

'But what about the Grublins?' said Albert.

'I'll find a way through. Don't worry. I can be quite persuasive when I want to be!'

Yeah, I thought, I bet you can!

'Are you sure you'll be okay?' said Bessie.

I tutted and mimicked behind her back. She was being way too sugary. I mean, we hardly knew Martha after all.

'Yes, I'll be fine!' said Martha. Her tone was abrupt and short but seeing Bessie's injured expression she swiftly changed. 'Let's meet up inside Grublin City,' she said sweetly, 'and bring the Moshtikes. We may need them as reinforcements.'

'Well, at least let's fly with you to the border,' said Bessie in her cutest forgiving voice. 'The gnarled tree is just beyond there.'

With Gilbert the smell leading the way we flew swiftly towards the borders of Great Molaring still, thankfully, under the cover of darkness. Bessie kept to Martha's side all the way, chatting and giggling with her. Albert took to the other side nodding his head and laughing in all the right places. I tagged on behind – alone.

It wasn't long before we came across our meeting point where Edie and Fred stood waiting on one of the trees twisted branches.

'And about time too!' whispered Fred, pulling me round the back of the tree. 'We've been here for ages.'

'Hell, what's your problem?' I said, pushing his arm away.

'Look!' He pointed to the city gates as Edie grabbed Bessie and Albert and threw them roughly against the tree trunk.

'Bloody hell, what are they doing?' I said, peeping cautiously over a broken branch.

'We're not sure. Covered carts, pulled by waspies, keep going in and out.' Fred leant over the branch with me.

'W-W-What's in them?' said Bessie, from behind the tree. The quiet crumpling of brown paper indicated that another Grublin phobia attack was imminent. Edie went to her rescue, saying soothing words to calm her down.

'We're not sure,' said Fred.

'Sounds to me like you're not sure of anything!' I said crossly.

'Oh, you're wrong there, Aggie. I'm sure they've got Myrtle and the twins in there. We just heard two Grublins laughing about three pilp collectors helping with enquiries.'

'I'll give them …' My immediate instincts were to rush out from the tree and attempt to rescue Myrtle and the twins – Fred pulled me back though.

'Look for all we know, they've got extra troops in those carts.' Fred had his serious look on. 'We can't risk losing another one of us.'

'Fred's right, Aggie and we do have another way through now.' Albert looked around. 'Where's Martha?'

'Oh, do you mean that fairy going through the city gates!' said Fred, full of admiration. 'Crikey, they didn't even stop her.'

'Well, she said she could be quite persuasive,' puffed Bessie, removing her head from the brown bag.

'Yeah,' I said sarcastically, 'probably something along the lines of, 'I'm Arty's mother, let me in or he'll have you killed' – that would do it for me!'

A horrid smell wafted under my nose in protest at my unkindness towards Martha.

'Change back, Gilbert. We need to figure out our

next move.' Fred flicked the smell away with the back of his hand this time catching Gilbert's ear perfectly as he changed back to fairy form.

'Huh! Got you back,' snapped Bessie. Gilbert poked out his tongue then rubbed his ear.

We all gathered round the back of the tree, then huddled together in a small crevice in the distorted tree trunk.

'Look we know they're in there. Let's just sneak in and get them,' I whispered, impatiently. 'We've wasted too much time already. Poor Myrtle will be terrified.'

'We can't just *sneak* in, can we?' said Fred.

'Well,' said Bessie, 'what if Edie went all invisible, like. She could go in and see if Myrtle and the twins are okay.'

'Oh, I'm sorry but I'm still trying to control the power,' said Edie sadly. 'I could probably get in but I don't know if I'd get out again.'

'I just want to take her home,' I said, trying hard to control my tears.

Albert put his arm on my shoulder. 'I want her back too …'

'… and the twins!' cut in Edie.

Albert corrected himself. 'And the twins – but after all the flying around from one place to the next, let's take our time and get it right. At least we know where she – they – are. Let's get the Moshtikes to help.'

'They won't do it for nothing,' said Fred, looking worriedly at Edie.

'We'll see,' she said. 'Perhaps we can strike a bargain with them.'

'Right – to Belcham Bog then,' I said. 'Land of the bog dwellers!'

********

Now Belcham Bog was not a place you went to voluntarily. More likely you went there if you were kidnapped, stumbled accidentally into it or had to go there for a dare. Hmmm, now where had I heard that before! This was purely because its inhabitants, the Moshtikes, were just so horrible. As former Grublins they obviously still had a lot of Grublin throwback in them! Of their many attributes, their vulgarity was probably the worse. These creatures weren't just verbally rude. They were physically rude too! They thought nothing of letting out their 'body gases' while you were standing there! Yuk! Talk about an appropriate place name – Belcham!

Unfortunately, they were probably the only creatures that could and would help us out because they hated the Grublins just as much as us. It was all to do with the feud …

'So what's it all about – this feud?' said Bessie as we passed over the treacherous swamp that lay just before the bog. It hissed and spat as we passed, trying to knock us out of the air with spurts of heated air.

'Careful – this swamp's been known to catch many a creature as it passed over,' I said.

'But what about the feud?' said Bessie, impatiently.

'Oh, it started about thirty years ago. The Moshtikes were actually Grublins to start with ...'

'Oh, bloody hell. They're related to Grublins ... and you're taking us there! I'm sorry but I have enough problems coping with Grublins as it is ...'

'They're not Grublins now, Bess. They've evolved!' I said, knowingly. 'Now do you want to know or what?'

'Assertive,' whispered Fred to Edie.

'Bossy more like!' said Bessie.

I ignored the remarks and carried on explaining the feud. 'Anyway, thirty years ago there weren't any Moshtikes just Grublins. Apparently, one of the Grublins secretly fell in love with a female pilp collector.'

'Oh now I know you're making it up,' said Gilbert. 'That's just too gross to happen!'

'But they smell awful,' agreed Fred. 'And what about all those nostrils, huh?'

'Well they say love is blind!' I said.

'And she must have been! Oh, this story stinks – just like a Grublin!' groaned Gilbert.

'Look, if you don't want to listen then sod off.' I turned to Bessie and carried on with the story. 'That didn't go down well with the Grublins at all. When they found out they told him to give her up or leave the city.'

'Aaahhh,' yawned Gilbert. 'Such an exciting story. I don't think.'

'Take no notice, Aggie,' said Fred, as he shoved Gilbert over to Edie who grabbed Gilbert's left leg and held on to it firmly. 'Carry on – did he give her up?'

I hesitated slightly then continued. 'Yeah but the Grublins were so mad at him that they chased him, his family and his friends out of the city.'

'But that doesn't explain how they became stinking bog dwellers, does it?' said Gilbert. 'What a stupid story!'

'I haven't finished, you twit!' I said. 'They'd searched for somewhere to settle and eventually found the bog.'

'Cor, you'd have thought they'd have looked just a little bit harder, wouldn't you? I mean fancy going from one hell hole to another,' said Gilbert.

'There wasn't anywhere else left,' I said, gritting my teeth.

'So what happened to the pilp collector?' said Fred.

I thought for a moment, trying to recollect what

I'd been told. 'That's funny – Ferrett didn't say,' I said.

'And so the Moshtikes adapted to their surroundings?' said Edie.

'Yep. They've lost their wings and two nostrils ... but not the smell. They still stink!' I wrinkled my nose.

'So the pilp collector – she could still be alive then?' said Edie.

'Well, yes. I suppose so.' I put a hand over my mouth. 'I'm sorry Edie,' I mumbled. 'But the smell is getting worse. I can hardly breathe.'

I looked around at the others and saw that they too were experiencing breathing difficulties.

The gases that rose and fell beneath us were truly vile and most unpleasant. They bubbled and burst, spraying their foul odour freely amongst us.

'Ohhh! That's just disgusting,' I said, as the largest, roundest bubble of all collapsed inwards producing the worst stench I'd ever encountered. I held my hand tighter over my mouth. 'It's re-re-revolting ...' I fought to finish the sentence but my mouth wouldn't form the words my brain had chosen. Then an eerie voice wandered unannounced into my mind.

*'Don't try to fight it. Just relax.'*

I tried to look round at the others but found my self slipping in and out of consciousness yet I didn't fall. I just drifted lightly onto the surface of the swamp below where a small boat was waiting.

*'Try to stay calm while your gills are attached.'*

Try to stay calm while my GILLS ARE ATTACHED! 'A – aa – arr – rgg – hh,' I couldn't even scream properly but I think the message was clear. I was not happy! I struggled as my hands were held down and something was placed around my neck.

As I tried to scream again, the voice in my head spoke softly, reassuring me. *'It's okay. You're going into the water now. Just breathe normally.'*

As I hit the water my mind became clearer, unlike the water itself! I held my breath as I looked around for Fred, Bessie and the others, too frightened to breathe out again. But soon I was desperate for a gulp of air. *'Just open your mouth slowly. Let your gills do the work,'* said the voice.

Little by little I willed my lips to part allowing the water to seep into my mouth. As I took the breath I'd been waiting for I felt my neck expand as the air passed through the gills. The feeling of panic passed as I grew accustomed to my breathing.

From out of the reeds came a familiar sight swimming towards me. 'Oh, thank portals you're alright,' said Bessie, hugging me tightly. 'Isn't this brilliant? I've never been able to swim before and now look at me – *wheeeeee.*'

'She's a little excited,' said Albert, emerging from

the same reed bed, followed by Fred, Edie and Gilbert.

'Talking underwater too – how does that work?' Bessie added as she whizzed by.

'It's called magic, Bess. Perhaps you might have heard of it!' Sometimes I really did wonder where she kept her brain!

'So what happens now?' said Fred, watching Bessie turn somersaults in the water.

I elbowed him sharply in the side, 'Bloody hell, look – I think they're coming for us!'

Swimming directly towards us was a group of creatures, presumably Moshtikes. They bore little resemblance to their Grublin ancestry but were scary in a different way. Between their fingers and toes, webbing had formed and from their necks three clear lines of gills could be seen. Long matted hair took over faces and heads, while nails on hands and feet had grown to prize-winning lengths. Unkempt and unclean, the Moshtikes were head turners for all the wrong reasons.

With no chance of escape there was little we could do but keep still as they hovered around us, smelling our hair with their only nostril and pulling at our clothes. Bessie's antics ground quickly to a halt once she too had seen our welcoming party.

'You're to come with us. Belcher said so,' said the first one and presumably the leader of the gang. He spat noisily, finishing with 'Aaahh, that's better. Been trying to bring that up all day.'

Oh yuk! Too much information!

Behind him an assortment of misfits mimicked his disgusting behaviour by spitting, picking noses and eating long strings of ear wax pulled from each other's ears.

'Oh – my – portals, savages. That's what they are, savages!' whispered Edie.

'Ssshh! We need their help,' I whispered back.

The leader must have overheard. He pushed his face into Edie's. 'Savages, ay? I'll give you savages!' He grabbed her roughly by the arm and started swimming off. The others followed suit, each grabbing one of us on either side.

'Aaaarrgghh! Get off!' I shouted, the bubbles pouring from my mouth.

'Leave her be,' screamed Albert, trying desperately to get to me.

Gilbert seemed to be the only one not struggling to escape. His eyes were closed as if concentrating on something else.

Fred, still trying to wriggle out of the Moshtikes grip, yelled across to him. 'What are you doing?'

'If I could just change back ...' But it was no use, his power to become a smell again had been rendered useless by the water. 'I can't seem to do it – I suppose I'll just have to suffer like you lot.' He hung his head, miserably accepting his fate.

We were pulled and prodded towards a large cave that sat firmly on the floor of the bog. The outside was completely covered in algae which glistened when the light from the surface hit it. Tall, thin reeds grew up from the bottom, twisting and turning in the current as they framed the caves mouth. Small, chiselled holes in the rock allowed some meagre rays of light to filter in, giving us the smallest preview of what was inside.

Pulling Edie behind him, the leader of the misfits swam into the cave, his trusty followers – with us in between – followed closely. As my eyes grew accustomed to the dark I began to look around. Still somewhat bewildered, I was able to take in the contents of the long dark corridor. Tiny spiral fluorescent snails clung to the walls while thin snake-like creatures wriggled along the ground. The floor sloped upwards causing the water to drain and gave way to a higher dry platform where we all finally landed.

'Argh – ahem.' I took my first lungful of air since we'd entered the dreaded bog. 'So this is how you survive, huh!' I wrung some of the bog water out of my hair. It stank!

'Bloody hell,' cried Albert, spewing bits of green from his mouth. 'This is madness.'

'But I can swim … and talk underwater!' mumbled

Bessie under her breath as she squeezed and pulled at her dress. 'Not been able to do that before!'

It never ceased to amaze me at what was important to some fairies at times like this! Still, it had kept her mind off the Grublins at least.

At the far corner of the platform Edie was fussing over Gilbert who, despite putting on a brave but miserable face, was having real problems breathing again. He started to shiver and shake with the cold.

'Move through,' said one of the misfits. 'The heating room will dry you out. Move now.'

'Such pleasant company we seem to keep nowadays,' sighed Fred.

I looked at him and sighed back. 'I hope you don't mean me, Fred Trickle!'

He feigned a smile then attempted to flatten his hair down. As always, the crown tuft flicked straight back up, refusing to lie down for anyfairy – or Moshtike.

When the heating room had done its trick we were ushered into a vast hollowed out chamber where many Moshtikes were already gathered and waiting.

'Why are you here?' came a deep growling voice from above us. 'You are not welcome amongst us 'savages'. We despise pilp collectors almost as much as we despise the Grublins.'

Our misfit leader pointed to a well worn sign, *'Tresparsers will bee eetan.'*

'That's a bit harsh, isn't it?' I said out loud.

'Savages, see!' said Edie quietly.

'And they can't spell!' added Gilbert, drearily.

'SILENCE!' said the voice.

'But I thought you were happy for us to be here.' I said. 'Someone spoke … in my head …'

'Well you're wrong!' The voice grew nearer as the owner was lowered down into the centre of the room on a large platform. 'That was just a welcome gas, nothing more. We've had plenty of time to manipulate the many gases here for our own uses.'

As the platform touched the floor, the Moshtike leapt off and took his place behind a huge long table where other presumably important Moshtikes sat waiting. He slammed his hand down hard making us jump backwards.

'I-I-I'm sorry,' I spluttered. 'It's just that somefairy has kidnapped my sister.' Edie threw me a glaring look. ' – and the twins. And we can't get into Grublin City on our own. We can't offer you much but Martha reckoned you'd help us and …'

Before I could finish, the whole room erupted and cries of 'Martha, Martha' echoed around the chamber.

Albert looked across at me and shrugged his shoulders. Bessie could offer no explanation either.

At the table the angry Moshtike leant forward into the light, his face contorted as he sniffed then spat to the side of his chair. 'Martha, huh! She's back then is she?'

'Well, yeah. She told us to come and find you … you know her?' I said, warily.

'You could say that, yeah!' He laughed heartily, thumping the table several times with his fist.

He was being very cagey with his answers but I decided not to push him too far. We needed the Moshtikes help if we were to get Myrtle and the twins back and at last it looked as if the end to the dreadful events was in sight.

I took a deep breath to steady my nerves then shouted high above the crowd. 'So you'll help us then?'

'We'll go to Grublin City with you, yeah.' He beckoned for quiet before continuing. 'There are some old Grublin *friends* I'd like to have a few words with.'

'Great!' I said triumphantly.

Bessie leant in and whispered, 'But he didn't say he'd help us.'

'Well no, not exactly but that's what he meant – I think.'

# Chapter Thirteen

We waited in the chamber while Belcher, as his name turned out to be, ordered the other Moshtikes around. Some ran across to a supply chamber where they stocked up with food and drink, filling little waterproof backpacks to the brim. Others collected weapons from a deep gash in the rock wall. Spears and swords were passed out one by one to those queuing up outside. I looked at my watch – again.

'Here, have a drink while you wait.' One of the Moshtikes threw some welcome bottles of juice our way to keep us hydrated.

'How much longer?' sighed Gilbert. 'She could be dead by the time we get there!'

'Shut up. That's the last thing we want to be thinking about,' said Fred, angrily.

But Gilbert was right. We really did need to be getting to Grublin City – hopefully, for all my doubts about her, Martha would have spoken to Arty and everything would be sorted out when we got there. And if it hadn't – we had the Moshtikes. Now that's what I call a back up plan!

'We are ready now,' said Belcher, his Moshtike army standing firmly behind him. It looked impressive.

Belcher led his men down the long corridor to

the water. As we followed the eerie voice reappeared in my head. *'Take a deep breath then let your gills take over.'*

I took a huge lungful of air just as we came to the slope then jumped into the water. The others followed except for Bessie who seemed to have a sudden and unexpected dose of water fright.

'Come on, Bess,' called Albert. 'I'll wait for you.'

Amazingly her fears disappeared at once and she jumped straight into Albert's waiting arms. He held her hand as they swam together. Yuk!

I swam to catch up with Fred who was following hard on the footwebs of the Moshtikes. 'So we just follow them, huh?'

'Well,' he said, 'we need to wait until we get back on dry land. I'm not sure how they're going to survive up there.'

But he needn't have worried for as soon as we emerged from the bog, the Moshtikes began to adapt to their surroundings – again. As they reached the surface each one lay on their fronts and waited. Before long, tiny wings began to push through their backs, flapping frantically as they were dried and tested.

'I thought you said they'd lost their wings,' whispered Albert as we witnessed the extraordinary event.

I shrugged my shoulders. 'That's what I was told – by Ferrett.'

When each was ready they took off from the water, sweeping and swishing around. Then finally the Moshtike's gills retracted back into their necks leaving just a dull orange spot where they once had been.

There was no heating room out here, of course, so we just flew around quickly in order to dry out.

'So, Grublin City's still in the same place, yeah?' growled Belcher.

What I wanted to say was; no, it was moved to another part of Mirvellon by the preservation of Grublins society so it could be marvelled at by future generations! What I actually said was, 'Yes, it is.'

'Right then. Let's go!' As he shouted, hoards of Moshtikes took to the skies, flapping their tiny wings frantically. But what about the plan!

'Er, excuse me Mr Belcher.' He stopped in mid-flight, his wings pulsing gently. 'Shouldn't we talk about what we'll do when we get there?' I stepped back as he hovered directly in front of me. The airborne Moshtikes tuned their wings to pulse and waited.

'I mean, I need to find my sister and the twins – in one piece'. I looked at their heavy hoard of spears and swords in dismay. 'And you, well you all look like you're going for full on war.'

'Do you want us to come or not?' he said, pushing his face into mine.

'Well, yeah.'

'Right – to Grublin City then.' He took off again. The others immediately fell in behind him.

'So they'll help then?' said Bessie.

'I think they will,' I said, feeling very unsure of the situation. With Belcher unwilling to commit, I wondered if I'd just be better blowing the whistle again. I played with it in my pocket, watching as the swarm of Moshtikes flew overhead.

'You can't blow it again – not yet,' said Edie, reading my thoughts. 'It has to be an absolute emergency. Dire consequences – remember?'

'This is ridiculous! I have a magic whistle which could save Myrtle but I can't use it,' I screamed angrily. 'And all that stupid nonsense about 'dire consequences'. Well, where the hell are they?'

Gilbert pointed to my neck. 'Dire consequences!' he said.

'Er, hem. No Gilbert. Th-Th-They're gills,' said Fred, then added quickly, 'and very nice they are too!'

I felt around my neck and sure enough, the three clear lines of gills were still attached to my neck. 'But these come off. Don't you remember how they were stuck on when we arrived at the bog?' I looked around at the others. They were all gill-less. I felt my neck again. The outlines of the attachment had disappeared completely – just the three gill lines protruded. 'Oh, my portals! I've still got gills?' I sighed. 'I blew that bloody whistle for Martha. She should suffer the consequences not me.'

'B-B-But think how useful they could be ...' muttered Bessie.

Oh, I didn't have time for all this! The gill problem would have to wait. I'd pay the healers a visit and they'd sort it out – hopefully! But for now – Grublin City.

Growling and muttering under my breath, I took off after the Moshtikes. Edie caught up with me and tried to offer reassurances while Gilbert flew alongside curiously inspecting the three lines that now occupied a permanent position on either side of my neck.

After a while, my mind settled and I began to focus on Myrtle – and the twins. How would we find them? Where would Gertie Cruet be? Then an awful thought crept into my mind – was all this trouble really just to get back at me? But with Grublin City now firmly in our sights I pushed those worries away to the back of my mind and refocused.

Bessie began to shake and quiver as we made our approach. With no brown bags left there was little we could to do help her. Edie talked to her calmly telling her to put her fears away and bring the anger forward.

'Arrgghh! Let me at 'em.' It seemed to work – too

well. Bessie sped down to the front of the Moshtike swarm and sidled up to Belcher.

'Hell, it's either one way or the other with her,' I said.

'Hmmm,' said Gilbert, still inspecting my gills.

The putrid gases of the city leapt out to greet us as we made our final descent, surging through our mouths and noses – and my gills! The River Grub gurgled noisily around the walls, rising and falling, spurting bubbles as it hit the ground. It was an eerie thing to be back here so soon but at least this time we had back up. As we came in to land, beside the gnarled old tree, we looked around for ways of entering.

'Hey, that's weird!' said Albert.

'Oh, don't you start!' I rubbed the gill marks on my neck vigorously.

'No, I mean no guard on the gate.'

'Now that's really weird.' I turned to Belcher. 'There's always a Grublin on the gate.'

'Perhaps they're expecting us,' he said. 'Let's go and see.'

'Don't forget about Myrtle ... and the twins.' I called after him as he and his army surged towards the gate.

'Aren't we going with them?' said Bessie, for once eager to get in amongst the Grublins. 'I'll pulverise them, I will.'

'Stop it! You sound just like one of them,' I pointed to the last Moshtike who disappeared beyond our view as he flew through where the guard should have stood.

We waited for about ten minutes then tentatively flew towards the city wall. Albert took the lead, holding Bessie behind his arms in case she made a foolish turn. In her present state that was highly likely!

'Keep behind me,' whispered Fred to Gilbert and Edie. I tucked myself in somewhere in the middle. Approaching the gate, my heart hammered and a shiver whizzed up and down my spine. I swallowed hard, trying to build up courage for what was to come. We slid in quietly, edging up against the wall so as not to be seen. Dark shadows loomed everywhere and lights from the gas lamps danced around as if just waiting to give us away.

There was no sign of the Moshtikes or, come to that, any Grublins. The main area was deserted. The only visitor was dark dense fog which flowed up and down the alleyways, only dispersing as it hit the ground.

'Where are they?' grunted Bessie. 'Where are the nasty little bleeders?'

'Not the time, Bess, really.' I squished myself past Albert to look around the corner. Ahead was a row of buildings, leaning all over the place – typical

Grublin builds. Faint glows were emitted from holes in their walls – someone must be in! At the very end stood 'Meltiess Mettell Werkss', the infamous factory where we last confronted Arty Granger and the Grublins. It brought back horrific memories.

'Slide past and get to the end where the mettell werkss are,' I said.

Gilbert froze. 'But that's where Victor saved us – when he was good ...' He looked sadly down the row at the factory.

'Come on we've got to make a fly for it – now!' We dashed along the walls, avoiding the light holes at all costs, ending swiftly at where it had all started – the roof of the factory. We landed gently and in silence. Looking around there was still no sign of Grublin life. It was all very peculiar!

Suddenly, out of the night sky dropped a herd of creatures, each one as ugly as the next. Spitting and growling and holding ... spears and swords – Moshtikes.

Pushing my heart back into position from my stomach, I managed to babble a few words. 'Have you found her – and the twins?'

Belcher stepped forward. 'No, we ain't.'

'Oh, hell ...' I sighed, feeling for the whistle.

'We ain't found nothing. There ain't no Grublins here or pilp collectors. No one – nothing!'

'You mean, nothing at all?' said Edie. 'Oh no, those

poor chids. Wherever can they be?' Her hankie reappeared and predictably, she buried her face in it.

All of a sudden a cry came up from the back of the crowd. 'Belcher, Belcher. I found one huddled up under the wood pile. Look, look.'

The crowd parted as one of the Moshtikes pushed through with a Grublin attached to his hand.

'Tell us what you know, Grublin,' screeched Belcher.

'Il nott sayingg nothingg!' spat the Grublin. He crossed his arms in defiance. 'Nothingg youu doo orr sayy willl makee mee grasss themm upp.'

'Hang on a minute. Isn't this the Grublin from the last battle?' Bessie walked around the Grublin eyeing him up and down. 'You know, the one we cornered and felt sorry so I let it go.' It was now the Grublins turn to swallow hard.

'And didn't I say at the time that … ' she poked it in the chest, 'you would owe me a favour for that – didn't I?'

'Errgghh,' squealed the Grublin.

'Pay back time, matey!' whispered Bessie in his ear. 'Now tell us what we want to know or I'll find another broom handle and give you what for.'

'Okayy,okayy – keepp herr offf mee.'

With great reluctance he told how the Grublins had moved everything out and gone somewhere new.

'Did you see my sister? Did you see the twins?' Albert shouted.

'II onlyy kneww theyy weree movingg outt. II wass supposedd too goo withh themm butt II drunkk tooo muchh plumm branddy lastt nightt andd didn'tt hearr themm goo.'

'What about Gertie Cruet? Did you see her?'

The Grublin pulled a face to show he's no idea who we were talking about.

'She's got a long pointy face, dreadful hair and a bad temper,' said Gilbert.

'Shee wass heree lastt nightt withh herr threee friendss – andd Marthaa.' The Grublin recoiled in horror as Albert jumped on him.

'They weren't her friends they were the pilp collectors we've been looking for!' he screamed in the Grublins face.

I pulled him off, aware of the eerie silence that fell when Martha's name was mentioned. The Moshtikes looked at each other and started to mumble. 'Martha was here. Martha was here.'

But their mumblings didn't deter Bessie. She was still under the 'spell' Edie had put on her.

'And Arty Granger? Where's he then?' screeched Bessie.

The Grublin flinched. 'He'ss stilll att Murshamm Marshess, isn'tt hee? Hee hasn'tt beenn heree.'

'What? That's rubbish. The two Grublins we saw

in Spercham said he was back,' said Fred. 'They said Arty was after us – for revenge.'

'Itt can'tt bee himm – he'ss stilll groundedd.'

Completely confused, I tried to carry on the conversation. 'So where have the Grublins gone – where's this new land?'

The Grublin hung his head down low. 'II don'tt knoww, reallly, II don'tt knoww.'

Bessie grabbed him by the hair. 'You're lying. Now tell us where they've gone!'

'Okayy, okayy.' He muttered something under his breath.

Albert prodded him with his foot. 'What? What did you say? Speak up!'

'Pilpsvillee – that'ss wheree they'vee alll gonee, Pilpsvillee.' He fell back on the ground, laughing hysterically.

'You've been stalling us you horrible beast, haven't you?' Albert leapt on the Grublin again and struck him several times around the head.

After a few minutes Belcher yanked Albert off but not before giving the Grublin a hefty kick to the leg.

'Get out of here before I set my family on you,' he shouted as the Grublin limped away into a corner. He sat there sniggering.

The immediate reaction to the Grublin's revelation was silence. We had been led away from our own land purposefully. I fingered the soft wood of the whistle deciding whether to blow on it or not.

Edie crept up behind me disturbing my thoughts once more. 'Just wait, Aggie,' she sniffed. 'Wait a little longer – until you have no choice.'

Removing my hand from my pocket, I refocused on the task ahead. 'How long since they left?' I shouted over to the Grublin.

'Justt afterr Marthaa arrivedd,' he snorted.

I thought for a moment then realised there was only one way forward. 'Pilpsville then.'

'But it will be a trap,' said Albert.

'It's just the Grublins though. Arty's not there to lead them is he?' I turned to the sniggering Grublin who nodded. 'Judging by the last battle, all we need are a few broom sticks and mops and it'll all be over.'

'The Moshtikes will come in handy too!' said Bessie.

'Yeah, let's hope so.' With that we took off, leaving the stalling beast of Grublin far behind.

The Moshtikes were more than eager to stay with us. In fact when Martha's name had been mentioned again, there was much jostling and grunting amongst them.

We passed back over the sparkling roofs of Great Molaring, through to three-storied Premolam and eventually to our home town, Insisorton. Along the way, the only thing we had encountered was the lingering stench of the Grublins that had gone ahead. An unnatural silence had swept over the towns and not a single living creature was visible.

We flew straight towards the pilp plant, the centre of the pilp collecting world. The quietness of the streets echoed in my ears. I'd never known it like this. So quiet, so still.

'Look down there,' called Gilbert. 'It's Martha!'

Sure enough, just outside the pilp plant doors stood Martha, all alone.

The Moshtikes sighed and grunted.

'Come down,' called Martha to us all. 'Don't be afraid. It's all okay.'

On hearing that, Bessie, Fred and the others started to drift down. I was a little more reluctant. Doubts ran through my head again. Why was she alone? Where were the Grublins?

'Come on, Aggie. It's Martha,' called Albert.

I landed cautiously next to Fred. Martha beckoned us all inside. 'Let's go through to the office. There's someone you all know in there.'

At last, I thought, Myrtle!'

'Let's make it a surprise,' she said, walking on tiptoes, her finger pressed firmly to her lips. We followed closely behind, ready at last, to welcome Myrtle back.

Although the pilp plant had huge windows, the office at the back had just a tiny pane of glass to let the light through. As we entered the room, a dark figure stood peering at an old map of Pilpsville that hung on the wall. I wanted to run up and hug her but Martha pushed her finger even closer to her mouth. I'd just have to wait a little longer.

Martha crept up to where the figure stood, lost in it's thoughts. I crossed my fingers as she moved closer. She drew a deep quiet breath then tapped the figure on the back. 'Surprise!'

But far from being surprised, the voice that replied sounded shocked and horrified – and it wasn't Myrtle's.

'Who set you free? How?' The figure stepped forward and looked over to the doorway where we all stood. It was Ferrett Granger.

'You stupid, fairychids! You've really gone and done it now.'

I stood aghast. He looked totally distraught.

Bessie, as always Martha's strongest defender, came to her defence once more. 'How can you say that seeing as all we've done is shown you for what you really are, Ferrett Granger. A wicked, evil fairy who trapped a poor young girl into marriage for money then abandoned her to the human world.'

Ferrett sunk to the ground, his hands covered his face. He rocked to and fro as he repeatedly cried, 'What have you done? What have you done?'

I didn't know how to react to this. I'd so expected to see Myrtle but now seeing Ferrett like this upset me greatly. It was quite a shock to see a fully grown fairy of his age in such a state. I began to panic. 'This isn't right, Fred. Why's he behaving like this?'

'Ah, that might be because I told you a teensy, weensy lie.' Martha curled her hair around her finger in just the cutesy manner that Bessie often did. 'You see, *I* married Ferrett for *his* money but only after my true love was banned from seeing me.'

Two Moshtikes came from behind us and grabbed Ferrett roughly by the arms. Then in strode Belcher stretching out his webbed hand in front of her. He knelt down and kissed her hand. 'At last, my love,' she said, 'I have waited a long time for this moment.'

'Oh, yuk! You can't be serious!' I said, trying not to gag at this 'happy' reunion.

'Well, once Arty was born I had no need for Ferrett. I would train my son in the night arts and use those powers to revenge those who'd forced Belcher and I apart.' She stroked Belcher's head tenderly. 'But just as I was about to curse him, that naughty Ferrett read out the counter curse he got from the healers, leaving me stuck in the human world as a pilp donor. But now I'm back and I can pick up from where I left things.' She cast her arm around the room majestically then turned to face me. 'Oh, and by the way, it's goth not goff you stupid creature!'

'Why you.' I made a move to grab her but was quickly pulled back some other Moshtikes who had just appeared in the room.

'Thank you, my love,' said Martha, as Belcher took up position by my side. He smiled and tightened his grip on my arms. Moshtikes encircled Albert, Fred and Gilbert, throwing them back roughly behind the door.

Bessie, now quiet and bewildered, was led with Edie to join them. As they sat together, Edie's eyes rapidly changed colour several times. She snapped her fingers over and over but nothing happened. Either the power of invisibility had been lost or darker forces were at work.

My head spun as I now tried to unravel all the latest events, leaving me completely unprepared for the next one.

'Ah, mother, there you are. Everything okay?' Arty Granger strutted across the floor and kissed Martha on the cheek.

'Yes, my dear. Never better in fact. Your plan worked beautifully!'

'Naturally,' he smirked, then turned and laughed in my face. 'You could never leave things alone, dearie, could you? And once Gertie had kidnapped that sister of yours, on my behalf of course, well, I knew you'd follow the trail I'd set – eventually leading you to Martha – and the Moshtikes. By the way, those gills really suit you, dear!'

As he turned back to his mother, Edie caught my

eye. 'Blow the whistle,' she mouthed. 'Blow it now!'

I struggled to loosen my arms from Belcher's grip, willing my hands towards my pocket.

'Is this what you're looking for?' cried Martha in delight. 'Have you lost your little whistle, dear?' She held the wooden object high in her hand, waving it around for all to see.

'Give me that back. It was a present from my Pa.' I yelled, still restrained by Belcher.

'Well now it's a present for me.' She slipped it into her own pocket and patted it into place. 'And let's be honest, dear. No amount of storm troopers can help you now!'

Edie sighed and fell back against the wall in despair. Next to her, Gilbert's head sunk low and he appeared to be crying. Fred put an arm round to comfort him and as he did, Gilbert whispered something in his ear. Fred smiled and moved his arm away. They were up to something!

Suddenly a grating yet familiar voice filled the air. 'Arty? Arty, are you in Daddy's office?' Gertie Cruet flounced in the room, sneering and snarling as she passed. 'Oh, jolly good. The entertainment's arrived then,' she snorted. 'Ohh, great gills, Lichen.'

'I think they've got something of yours, dearie,' said Arty.

Gertie turned to Fred and sneered, 'Oh yeah! I'll take that!' She ripped the backpack from his shoulders. 'I've always wanted my own FFP!'

I struggled to get free but Belcher's hold was too strong. Fortunately, he couldn't stop my mouth. 'You're a traitor, Gertie Cruet, a dirty, stinking traitor. Do you really think he cares about you anyway?' I nodded towards Arty. 'He only cares about himself.'

'And his mother,' chipped in Martha, stroking his hair.

'Come, Gertie,' said Arty. 'I've got a little present for you.'

But before she could respond Gilbert piped up quickly. 'I've got something for you too!' And in an instant, before their startled eyes, he turned from pilp collector into his alter ego – the smell.

I watched, taking morbid delight as he encircled Gertie making her spin on the spot. Weaving in and out of her mouth and nose was a new trick though.

'Get him off me,' she screamed. 'Arty, help me!'

She fought desperately to control the violent gagging spasms she was now having. While all in the room just watched and stared – except me. I laughed my head off. Oh, how she deserved this and more, and I knew that the after effects would remain with her for a long while. But before long it all came to an abrupt end. Gilbert dramatically reappeared in his miserable fairy form.

'Why didn't you go?' said Fred as Gilbert was pushed once again into the corner. 'You could have escaped. You could have found help.' Fred thumped the wall angrily.

'I couldn't hold it any longer,' said Gilbert. 'Something felt strange – inside. '

Two of the Moshtikes helped a clearly distressed Gertie up from the floor. She held her head with one hand and her stomach with the other.

'Take her outside,' said Arty. 'until the smell wears off!' He waved his hand casually towards the door. 'She can have her 'reward' later.'

Arty turned his back on us showing clear evidence of his clipped wings which were still intact. He'd obviously been flown out of his marsh prison. He had one final blow to deliver, however. 'I trust you enjoyed the refreshments at Belcham Bog.'

Belcher sniggered. I looked over to where the rest of the gang were sitting. Already their facial features were being taken over and the colour of their skin grew greyer by the minute.

Ferrett gasped as he looked over, his hands now tightly bound. 'Arty leave them be. You've got what you want.' He nodded at Martha.

'Not quite, *father,* not quite!'

********

The central area around the community pilp plant was crammed full – with Grublins! On a pre- erected stage, the evil Arty Granger, Martha at his side, stood back, raised both hands in the air and admired his work. He threw back his head and laughed, 'At last, a world free of pilp collectors.'

'Whatt about mee, Artyy? Afterr all I've done forr youu!' The cries of Gertie Cruet rang out pitifully above the crowd.

'Ah, Gertie dear. I see you've drunk your reward already!'

'Butt you saidd it wouldd make mee speciall,' she screamed.

'And so it has, my dear.' He called over to a familiar Grublin. 'Take her back to the city. I've no use for her now,' he spat venomously.

'Yess, bosss,' said Meltiee, anxiously rubbing his hands together.

He gestured to a pair of Grublins standing idly by. They pulled the struggling Gertie, along with Violet and Petunia, over to a waspie cart which stood at the far end of the pilp plant.

'Okayy, alll gonee noww Bosss. Err, whatt shalll II doo withh thee restt off themm?'

'Load them all up and take them back to the mettell werkss – no wait, first bring me that meddling Lichen girl.'

At the back of the crowd, I sighed deeply, took a small step forward and accepted my fate. I clutched at the last remaining strands of straight black hair that had always defied all odds to curl it, as Meltiee the mettlee werkerr made his approach.

'Grabb herr!' he shouted to the two Grublins standing either side of me.

'Struggle all you like, dearie,' called Arty as I was dragged before him. 'There's no escape for you or any other fairy – ooops! I mean Grublin. Ha ha ha!'

'Butt whatt aboutt the human childrenn? They'll be expectingg a toothh fairy too collectt theirr teethh. It'ss what wee doo. It'ss howw we existt. Theyy believe inn uss!'

'So they do. So they do.' He cast his right arm out casually. 'Look around you dearie. Look closely at the new breed – of pilp collector.'

'B-B-Butt they're tooo clumsyy. They'll wakee the pilpp donorss.'

'Not at all. They'll collect the pilps … just like before.'

'II don't understand,' I said. 'What wouldd you gainn?'

'Well, I won't be wasting magic dust on those humans, that's for sure.'

'Butt you havee to – it'ss partt off the agreementt. Wee leave ourr magic dustt underr the pilloww and it changess into whatt the donorss wish forr.'

'But they only ever wish for those silly round metal discs – what a waste! No, we'll leave them something useful, something less valuable to us, something like a gallon of plum brandy.'

'Butt that'll attractt the spritess. Our worldss willl be turnedd upside downn. There'll bee chaoss.'

'Precisely – and the humans will blame the sweet little 'tooth fairy' won't they? Before long, tooth fairies will disappear completely from human memories.'

'But whatt aboutt the spritess – they'll attackk …'

'And the *Grublins* will defend the new principality of Grubland.'

'Principalityy?'

'Well, I toyed with calling it a kingdom but quite frankly, dearie, King Arty was just too vulgar – even for me. No, I shall head up the new land of the Grublins, with Grublin City as my seat of residence.'

'Bloodyy hell, you'vee really lostt the plott.'

'Maybe but who's going to stop me – you and your friends? Not this time – dearie! Take her away.'

Two familiar pairs of arms closed in around me. The crown tuft of one was just visible while the brown bushy plaits of the other had all but disappeared.

'Bessiee! Fredd! Stop itt, please!' I tried wriggling out of their grasp but they held fast. I gazed into their eyes. The glare was fixed. Their transformation complete.

'Welcome to your new life – enjoy the flight!' He beckoned to another Grublin holding a large grey bottle. As she brushed by me, a wisp of red wiry hair fell gently onto my arm. I clasped it tightly in my hand, closed my eyes and wished hard.

She stood nervously in front of me and thrust the grey bottle into my sweating hand. The huge Grublin eyes peered out desperately, pleading with me to save her.

To either side of her was a short, blonde haired Grublin. Together they gently stroked her skirt, trying to smooth out the many wrinkles. My eyes filled with tears as I slowly realised who they were.

I wound the wisp of red hair round and round my finger, hardly daring to speak. She gestured me to drink.

I looked up into her saddened face. 'Bugfacee? Iss thatt you?'

P.S. To translate from Spritespiel,

Just take the previous letter

in the alphabet!